publication of this book

in the South Caroliniana Series

was made possible by the generosity of

Jamie and Marcia Constance

Rab and Dab

THE SOUTH CAROLINIANA SERIES

1. *A Catalog of the South Caroliniana Collection of J. Rion McKissick*
2. *Selections from the Letters and Speeches of the Hon. James H. Hammond*
3. *The Poetry of William Gilmore Simms: An Introduction and Bibliography*
4. *A Divided Heart: Letters of Sally Baxter Hampton, 1853–1862*
5. *Indians of the South Carolina Lowcountry, 1562–1751*
6. *The Writings of Benjamin F. Perry, Volumes I–III*
7. *John Punterick. A Novel of Life in the Old Dutch Fork*
8. *The Charleston Book: A Miscellany in Prose and Verse*
9. *Rab and Dab*

Other titles in preparation

Series editor
JAMES B. MERIWETHER

Editorial Advisory Board
CLYDE N. WILSON
CHARLES E. LEE
E. L. INABINETT
GENE WADDELL

Elizabeth Allston Pringle

RAB AND DAB

edited
and with an introduction
by
Anne Blythe

THE REPRINT COMPANY, PUBLISHERS
SPARTANBURG, SOUTH CAROLINA
1985

The text of *Rab and Dab* was originally published as a serial in the *Atlantic Monthly,* November 1914–January 1915. It was first published in book form in 1984 by the Seajay Press, Northport, Alabama, in an edition limited to 126 copies. This is a trade reprint of that limited edition.

Introduction copyright © 1984 by Anne Blythe

Reprinted: 1985 with permission
The Reprint Company, Publishers
Spartanburg, South Carolina 29304

ISBN 0-87152-405-8
Library of Congress Catalog Card Number: 84-24887
Manufactured in the United States of America on long-life paper

Library of Congress Cataloging in Publication Data

Pringle, Elizabeth W. Allston (Elizabeth Waties Allston), 1845–1921.
  Rab and Dab.

  (The South Caroliniana series ; 9)
  "Text . . . originally published in serial form in the Atlantic monthly, November 1914–1915"—
  Reprint. Originally published: Northport, Ala. : Seajay Press, 1984.
  I. Blythe, Anne. II. Title. III. Series.
[PS2664.P82R3   1985]   813'.52   84-24887
ISBN 0-87152-405-8

CONTENTS

Acknowledgments	vii
Introduction	ix
Illustrations	xxiv
Rab and Dab	3
Epilogue	69
A Note on the Text	75

ACKNOWLEDGMENTS

My greatest debt is to James B. Meriwether, for it was through him that I first came to know Mrs. Pringle and her work. I am grateful for his high standards, his steadfast encouragement, his unfailing patience—and for the time which he so generously gave to this project and to me. His training and his guidance are invaluable and lasting gifts.

To Gene Waddell, Director of the South Carolina Historical Society in Charleston, South Carolina, where the Allston-Pringle-Hill papers are located, and to his staff, especially David Moltke-Hansen and Harlan Greene, I am also much indebted. Themselves interested in Mrs. Pringle and her writings, they have assisted me with my research in every way, and their pleasure in new discoveries has matched my own. I am particularly obliged to Mr. Greene for his help with the illustrations.

I wish to thank Kenneth A. Lohf, Librarian for Rare Books and Manuscripts at Columbia University, and his staff, for their assistance with my work upon the Pringle-Bancroft correspondence. Mrs. Pringle's letters to the historian are a valuable supplement to the Allston-Pringle-Hill Collection. Thanks are due also to the staff of the Manuscripts Division, Library of Congress, where the Owen Wister correspondence is held.

Finally, it is a pleasure to acknowledge the assistance of Elizabeth Holland, publisher of the Seajay Press, and Thomas E. Smith, publisher of the Reprint Company, who made it possible for *Rab and Dab* to become a book at last.

A.B.

INTRODUCTION

Elizabeth Allston Pringle is best known for the book *A Woman Rice Planter,* which she wrote under the pen name "Patience Pennington," and which was published in 1913 with an introduction by Owen Wister. Wister calls it "a Southern picture unsurpassed" and "a native document of permanent historic value."[1] He knew Mrs. Pringle, and was familiar both with her life and her writings. He had delighted in the stories she told of her place and her people, and had urged her to write them down. He felt that she combined rare artistry as a storyteller with an unusually rich store of experiences—experiences which she first recorded in journals and letters and ultimately, with his encouragement, would go on to expand and polish for publication.

Among these perhaps the best was the story of Rab and Dab, two little black orphans, which at one time she considered making into a small book,[2] but which was published only as a serial in the *Atlantic Monthly.* It appeared less than a year after the publication of *A Woman Rice Planter* and under the same pen name. Not long afterward she apparently considered publishing at least a brief epilogue to their story, but it remained in draft among her papers at her death in 1921, and the three serial installments of the original story have remained virtually unknown. The present volume, then, for the first time makes this work available in book form, as its author wished, and to it adds the first publication of the epilogue.

* * *

Born on May 29, 1845 at "Canaan Seashore," Pawleys Island, South Carolina, Elizabeth Waties Allston was the second daughter of Robert Francis Withers Allston and Adele (Petigru) Allston and the third of their five children to survive childhood.[3] Her father owned and cultivated thousands of acres of rice lands in the Georgetown District of South Carolina. One of the most capable and successful rice planters of his time, he was also widely known for his writings, especially on rice cultivation and sea coast crops.[4] A strict constitutionalist, staunch advocate of States' Rights, and devout churchman, Allston served in his state legislature for over twenty-eight years and was Governor of South Carolina from 1856 to 1858. He is the central figure in his daughter's memoirs, *Chronicles of Chicora Wood*—the plantation where she grew up—which was published the year following her death. There she described him as "the only person in the world in whom I had absolute faith and confidence. I had never seen him show a trace of weakness or indecision. I had never seen him unjust or hasty in his judgment of a person. . . . Never a sign of self-indulgence, or indolence, or selfishness."[5] Though she chides herself for not being more like him she proved, both in her life and in the way she wrote about it, that she was at least as remarkable a woman as he was a man.

Plantation life before the War, in her father's time, she recalled, required "method, power of organization, grasp of detail, perception of character, power of

Introduction

speech; above all, endless self-control."[6] But it would require even more after the War. Her father died in 1864 and though her mother assumed control and managed the plantations for a while, heavy debts and impossible taxes eventually forced her to auction most of the property. Of the 4000 acres of Allston land, all that could be claimed after the War was the widow's dower, Chicora Wood—890 acres.[7] The house, Elizabeth would recall in her memoirs, had been "torn to pieces,"[8] tools and equipment were worn out, provisions and livestock had been stolen or destroyed, and there were few hands left on the plantation to work. It is not surprising that given such conditions, so many planters left their lands to begin new lives elsewhere.[9]

Elizabeth Allston was among those who chose to stay and rebuild, although she could not return to the land immediately. Her mother, while struggling to retain the estate, opened a boarding school in Charleston in 1866 and Elizabeth was needed to help. Though reluctant and even rebellious at the thought of giving up her youth to teaching school, she soon found to her surprise and delight that she loved teaching and was good at it.[10] They ran the school successfully for nearly three years and were able to meet primary expenses and retain Chicora Wood; in 1869 Mrs. Allston was granted her dower and the family moved back to their plantation. On April 26, 1870, Elizabeth married John Julius Pringle and went to live at his family plantation, White House, twelve miles down the Pee Dee River from Chicora Wood. The six short years of their marriage were shadowed by debts that outgrew what they could produce on the land, and the marriage ended with Pringle's death from malarial fever in Charleston on August 21, 1876.[11]

After his death Elizabeth returned to Chicora Wood and helped her mother with the duties and management of her home plantation. In 1880 a bequest enabled her to buy the White House from the Pringle heirs, and in 1885 she began to manage it from Chicora Wood.[12] After her mother's death in 1896 she assumed control of both plantations, living at Chicora Wood, traveling daily the hour and a half distance between the two estates. She had one servant, Clarinda Lance (named "Chloe" in *A Woman Rice Planter* and *Rab and Dab*), whom she called "the comfort of my life . . . having made it possible, by her devotion and faithfulness, for me to live in the old home alone since my mother's death, with no white person within a mile or two . . . a friend as well as servant."[13] Mrs. Pringle would drive her buckboard between the two plantations, watching over the work at each, scolding and encouraging the hands, appealing to their pride in hard honest work, disciplining them when necessary, always having something little to hand them—a pear, a biscuit, a piece of candy—when they came up and spoke with her. She would cross the river with a load of rice or field equipment in a small boat rowed by her boatman, Elihu, unafraid of wind and waves when he was at the oars. Though plagued by "heat, worry . . . discouragement and continual effort,"[14] she would work from sunrise till dark overseeing the work in progress, at times taking the plough herself. Yet a quality she knew was essential to her being was, in her own words, "my power of enjoyment."[15] She was always prepared to be captured by the infinite beauty of sunset; exhilarated by the race home against the mounting fury of a September storm; or refreshed by a morning bicycle ride on her "wheels," thanking her Maker for

Introduction

the blessing of the fresh cool air in her face. She lived with the elements—wind, water, sun, rain—fighting them and rejoicing in them, meeting their challenge to live her life and do her work. She was not afraid of work. She believed that hard work dignified and gave one grace. She pitied those who had "never really worked" because they "will never reach the point of excellence and development that could have been attained, had he or she learned to put out the whole strength, either of mind or body on something."[16] Surely she was referring to more than her work as a planter, for we know that she wrote, and wrote continuously, from her girlhood. She early acquired the habit of keeping a diary, her mother reminding her to write daily the events of the day before. Later on friends and relatives, recognizing her talent, encouraged her to write stories based on material from her diaries. In 1885 the Charleston *News and Courier* published a series of women's recollections of the War;[17] to it Elizabeth Allston Pringle contributed excerpts from her diary of 1863–1865, including a graphic, detailed, but remarkably controlled description of Yankee troops ravaging her home—and an equally remarkable self-portrait of a young woman for the first time confronted with the worst of mankind.

Sometime after the War, she drafted a letter to the editor of the *Atlantic Monthly* inquiring whether he would be interested in "a series of papers called 'Studies in Black and White' . . . written by a woman from a South Carolina rice plantation." Badly in need of money, and aware of the curiosity being expressed in the North about the South, she wrote that "our lives are not as [yours are] and therefore may have some interest."[18] Beginning in 1903 excerpts from her current diaries were serialized in the New York *Sun* and reprinted in the *News and Courier.* These excerpts, revised and expanded, freshened with the remembered detail inherent in keeping a diary, became in 1913 *A Woman Rice Planter.* Always aware of a Northern audience, she continued to write stories, plays, and essays drawn from the facts of her life, though she was often dissatisfied with what she wrote, leaving much of it unpublished, sometimes unfinished, at her death.

Mrs. Pringle's work as a planter and her work as a writer were the twin driving forces in her life. From one came the material—simply, directly, and truly experienced; from the other came the interpretation, the need to communicate to others the importance of what she had learned from her life and the lives around her. In 1908 she said in a letter to historian Frederic Bancroft, "I have always felt that having lived through the transition period of my country, and felt and suffered intensely at each stage, I owed it to myself and [my sisters] to make some record of the passing years."[19] Her world was changing rapidly and profoundly and she was determined to recreate that change for us in her writings. But though she was always conscious of her significance as the historian of a particular time and place, hers was not so much the historian's as it was the artist's need to preserve, for posterity, her world and her people—and also herself.

At the heart of her best writing and of her response to life is her sense of art, her aesthetic. Scattered through her journals are her accounts of her reading; her critical analyses are done from the standpoint of one who is a writer herself, and knows it. As a musician, too, she is very conscious of her power to move an audience by her technique and artistry. She had been a superb dancer as a young woman—"when any one danced with me . . . they always wanted to dance with me again"—but in some ways she enjoyed more playing the piano while others danced. After the War, when there were many more women than men at the dances, she was joyful that "when ever I had no partner, *I could play.*"[20]

With characteristic but undue modesty she told Bancroft, "I have been so removed from all literary and critical surroundings . . . I have had no chance to cultivate the art [of writing], except in the long letters I have written in the twelve years I have lived entirely alone, and they have been just photographic accounts of my daily life and doings, with no idea of style or literary merit, simply what my sisters wanted to know."[21] She was a woman in the man's world of a plantation, doing a man's work but without a man's traditional habit of command and unquestioned authority. Therefore her effectiveness as manager of the plantation work force required a greater development of psychological insight and power to overcome this difficulty; thereby, too, she became a finer artist and a more profound interpreter of human nature.

She did not expect any part of life to be easy. She required no more from the people she supervised than she demanded from herself, and when she got less from them, she unhesitatingly increased her own load because the work had to be done. She dedicated *A Woman Rice Planter* to her father, "to whose example of self-control and Christian fortitude, I owe the power to live my life independent of externals"; he had believed in God's will and hard work, and so did she. She believed that in the end good will triumph over evil, and we will be rewarded for our trials. It was such power, and such belief, that enabled her to succeed against almost overwhelming odds, and to survive trials such as those she experienced when she assumed responsibility for two wretched, savage little orphans.

* * *

Although she gave them fictional names (as she did herself), we must not forget that Rab and Dab were actual people, and though in telling their story she used the fictional techniques that she had so carefully practiced, she was following closely, if selectively, actual events in their lives. Her correspondence reveals that Rab and Dab were, respectively, Robert (Bobs) Spivy and Jesse Spivy, Jesse being the elder.[22] She had given them Biblical names when she revised her journal for the New York *Sun* serial in 1903. In Jeremiah 35:7, the tribe of the Rechabites, led by Jonadab, son of Rechab, is described as a nomadic desert tribe: "Neither shall ye build house, nor sow seed, nor plant vineyard . . . but all your days ye shall dwell in tents, that ye may live many days in the land where ye be strangers." She gave the name of nomads, that is, to the orphans she took into her care in a place where they were strangers.

The children came into her life upon their mother's death. In her 1899 journal Mrs. Pringle recorded how she had knelt on the floor beside the dying black woman, who was "beyond earthly sights & sounds," and promised her that she would see to it that her two little boys were cared for. (See illustration.) Four months later they were in her care and she was providing for them. The house servants were horrified that she should "harber furriners" in the "yard," as they called the plantation grounds, and they shot glowering looks at her and the two dirty, half-starved, pygmy-sized children. Their father was from an African tribe that was despised by the Negroes on the former Allston lands. He had married one of the plantation women, but the family was distrusted and even ostracized by the rest of the hands. Like Mrs. Pringle, the plantation blacks all held a firm belief in the Christian God, but they were the first to condemn and reject the orphans, whom they considered pagan, and never fully accepted them because of their alien inheritance. They believed the little "furriners" were fit for the "debbil" himself, born and committed to a life of evil, ruled by the serpent. But Mrs. Pringle looked beyond the sins they committed and into their souls; then she set her mind to their education and reform.

For Rab and Dab temptation was irresistible. They stole chickens, biting their necks to kill them; they stole eggs, burying some, eating some, selling some; they aimed a roman candle at a rabbit, making a horse bolt, smashing up the buckboard and ruining harness and reins; they told lies glibly and smoothly; they even threatened to burn the big house with her and Clarinda in it. They sneaked out of their beds at night and roasted chickens under the house; they broke into the larder and ate up everything in sight; they were truant from school for weeks at a time; they loved to fight. The faithful Clarinda, who knew their proclivities best, said that "de only way to mek [dem] behave 'eself is to keep um stirrin'...." Mrs. Pringle agreed and put them to work.

And the boys could work, sometimes loved the tasks she put them to in the yard, gathering "bresh" in a little wooden wagon for the kitchen fire, carrying the mail, running errands. They would be good for a spell, but then they were horrid. And when they were horrid, they did seem to belong to the devil himself, as the servants complained. Mrs. Pringle tried to answer complaint with reason. She told Elihu that "they have to fight a heavier battle with the devil than either you or I and we must try to help them." She talked to the boys, explained to them why one does not steal, why one does not heedlessly kill animals; she chastised and disciplined; she told Bible stories in words they could understand; she had them christened. They would reform. But they always strayed back to their old ways. A lesser person would have surrendered them to their bleak fate—would have declared them too evil for redemption. Mrs. Pringle did not.

She requires the reader, though, to wrestle with the question of the nature of good and evil. She gives us in *Rab and Dab* a study in the eternal struggle between those opposing forces. Is evil a small boy cruelly destroying, "chunking" to death a beautiful bird? Is it a small boy killing a chicken, stuffing its warm body in his shirt and roasting it late at night under the house when the rest of the world is asleep? She does not resolve the question because she concerned herself with good, not evil. She wanted to help those two otherwise doomed children, and did. She did it with compassion and responsibility, with discipline and faith, with humor and enjoyment—and with patience.

At the beginning of *Chronicles of Chicora Wood*, musing upon the events of the "dark and tragic" years with which her memory is stored, she asks herself, "Shall I let all this die without a word?" It is a question she had already answered—in *A Woman Rice Planter;* in *Chronicles of Chicora Wood;* and when she realized the significance of her experience with those two orphans, and made it possible for us to share it by writing this book.

ANNE BLYTHE
Columbia, S.C.
23 September 1984

NOTES

1. "Patience Pennington," *A Woman Rice Planter,* New York: Macmillan, 1913. With an introduction by Owen Wister and drawings by Alice R. H. Smith. The quotations from the introduction appear on p. ix.
2. Elizabeth Allston Pringle to Frederic Bancroft, 28 January 1908. (Bancroft Collection, Columbia University Library.)
3. Margaretta P. Childs, biographical sketch of Elizabeth Allston Pringle in *Notable American Women 1607–1950: A Biographical Dictionary,* Cambridge: Harvard University Press, 1971, Vol. III, pp. 100–101.
4. J. H. Easterby, *The South Carolina Rice Plantation as Revealed in the Papers of Robert F. W. Allston.* Chicago: University of Chicago Press, 1945, p. 3. Easterby notes that Allston's *Memoir of the Introduction and Planting of Rice in South Carolina* (1843) "is still considered the best scientific treatise on the subject" (p. 3). Professor Easterby's work is still the most valuable single study of the Allston family and of the whole subject of rice planting in South Carolina.
5. Elizabeth W. Allston Pringle, *Chronicles of Chicora Wood,* New York: Scribner, 1922, pp. 210–211.
6. *Chronicles,* p. 78.
7. *Chronicles,* pp. 10–11.
8. *Chronicles,* p. 343.
9. George C. Rogers, Jr. *The History of Georgetown County, South Carolina.* Columbia: University of South Carolina Press, 1970, Chapter XX. Professor Rogers' history is invaluable for an understanding of the background of Elizabeth Allston Pringle's life and work.
10. *Chronicles,* pp. 340 ff. When not otherwise documented, biographical data are taken from *Chronicles of Chicora Wood.*
11. *News and Courier,* August 22, 1876, p. 4.
12. Childs, p. 100.

13. This is the description of her that appears in Chapter I of *Rab and Dab*. See also fn. 22.
14. *A Woman Rice Planter*, p. 206.
15. *A Woman Rice Planter*, p. 85.
16. *A Woman Rice Planter*, p. 114.
17. "Esther Alden" (Elizabeth W. Allston), "Fun in the Fort." This was originally published in the series "Our Women in the War" which ran in the *Weekly News and Courier* from 1884 to 1885 and was later published as a book: *Our Women in the War,* Charleston: *News and Courier* Book Presses, 1885. "Fun in the Fort" appears pp. 354–363.
18. Undated draft of letter to the editor of the *Atlantic Monthly*. (Allston-Pringle-Hill Collection, South Carolina Historical Society, Charleston, South Carolina.)
19. Elizabeth Allston Pringle to Frederic Bancroft, 12 July 1908.
20. *Chronicles,* pp. 305, 303, 304.
21. Elizabeth Allston Pringle to Frederic Bancroft, 12 July 1908.
22. From her diaries and letters it is possible to identify most of the people and places in *Rab and Dab*. "Chloe" is in reality Clarinda Lance; the real name of her "good man-of-all-work," Jim, is Joe. Chicora Wood becomes Cherokee; her summer pineland home, Plantersville, becomes Peaceville; White House, Casa Bianca; Georgetown, Gregory. However, in *Rab and Dab* Charleston, South Carolina and Asheville, North Carolina are referred to by their actual names.

The young niece who was with Mrs. Pringle at the time she assumed care of the orphans was probably Adele Van der Horst, the eldest daughter of Mrs. Pringle's sister, Adele (Della) Allston Van der Horst and Arnoldus Van der Horst of Charleston and Kiawah Island. Mrs. Pringle's diaries from 1899 to 1900 indicate that Adele, who was also her godchild, was with her at Chicora Wood for a prolonged visit. The "D." in the epilogue who gives Dab the small trunk to take to the Jenkins Institute and whose son meets Mrs. Pringle and Dab at the train station was Mrs. Van der Horst. The sister "L." in the mountains who, in the epilogue, asks to take Jonadab for the summer was Jane Louise (Jinty) Allston Hill, Mrs. Pringle's younger sister who was married to Charles Albert Hill, an Englishman. They, too, lived in Charleston but kept a summer home in the mountains of North Carolina. (Elizabeth Deas Allston, *Allstons and Alstons of Waccamaw,* Charleston:

Walker, Evans and Cogswell, 1936, p. 50.) The sister Mrs. Pringle asks to visit the Jenkins Institute for her and report what she thought of it was probably Mrs. Van der Horst. Mrs. Hill had no children and traveled frequently; Mrs. Van der Horst, with seven children (*Allstons and Alstons,* p. 49), spent most of her time in Charleston.

There are surviving letters from both of the Spivy boys (see illustrations) written between the years 1906 and 1908. There is also correspondence between the Reverend Jenkins and Mrs. Pringle in 1906, in which he thanks her for the money for Bobs's education and notes that he is glad that she is pleased with Jesse's progress. (Allston-Pringle-Hill Collection, South Carolina Historical Society, Charleston, South Carolina.)

JESSE AND ROBERT SPIVY ("DAB" AND "RAB")

Reproduced from a photograph tipped into the South Carolina Historical Society's copy of the 1914 second printing of *A Woman Rice Planter* (New York: Macmillan, 1913)

Elizabeth Allston Pringle at Boat Landing, Chicora Wood
Reproduced from frontispiece of *Chronicles of Chicora Wood*, Boston: Christopher House, 1940

Rab and Dab the Orphans
Extract from Diary of Patience Pennington
Peaceville Sept 22ᵈ 1899

Went down to Casa Bianca to rouse the hands to action, for we are to begin cutting rice in Marsh field tomorrow. I found the boy who blew himself up with gun powder two days ago in great suffering — Dressed his face and hands, using a feather to cover them with olive oil. He is a distressing object. I gave orders that every man, woman and child over twelve should be in the field tomorrow and promised to be down early myself.

Sept 23ᵈ Just as I was getting into the wagon early this morning, carrying linen rags and olive oil to dress Nero's burns and nourishment for him also lunch for myself, and a few pears and things to give to the hands, I saw a pitiful little black figure standing at the foot of the steps, it was Jonadab the little

FIRST PAGE OF THE MANUSCRIPT OF "RAB AND DAB THE ORPHANS"
From Allston-Pringle-Hill Collection

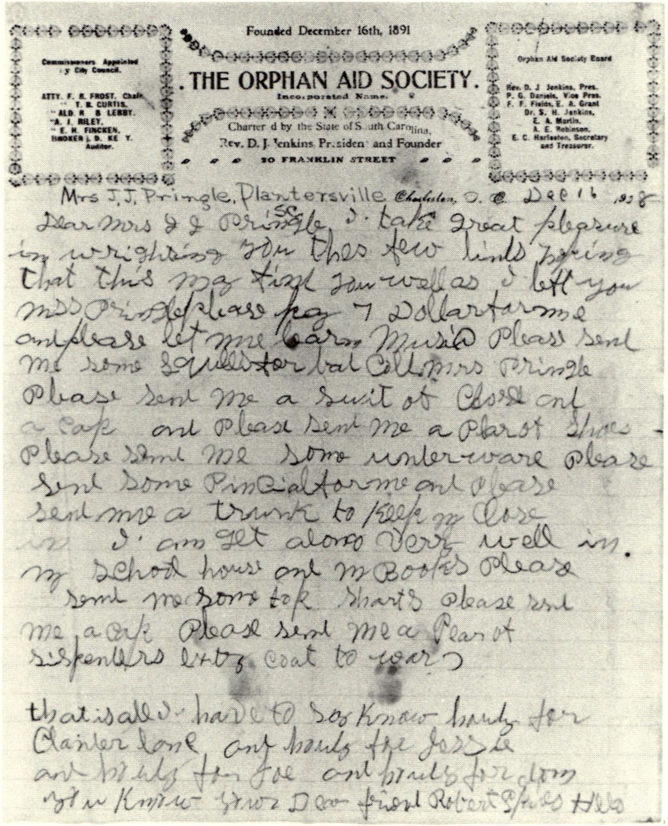

THE ORPHAN AID SOCIETY.
Founded December 16th, 1891.

Plantersville, Clarendon Co. SC Dec 16, 1908

Mr J J Pringle,

Dear Mr & Mrs Pringle, I take great pleasure in writing you this few lines hoping that this may find you all as it left me. Mr Pringle Please Sir I want you and Mrs Pringle to do something for me Mrs Sarahwashington Pringle Please send me Allston Pringle Please send me a suit of Clothes and Please send me a Pair of Shoes and Please send me Sum underware Please send Some Pinsil and Some Paper send me a trunk to Pack my clothes in I am getting along very well my school hours out my Books. Please send me a pair of short Please send me a pair of Short and Suspenders and a coat to wear. that will do so you must send me Clothes long enough and Buts for School so you must excuse for my Short letter

From your Dear friend Robert Spivy Rab

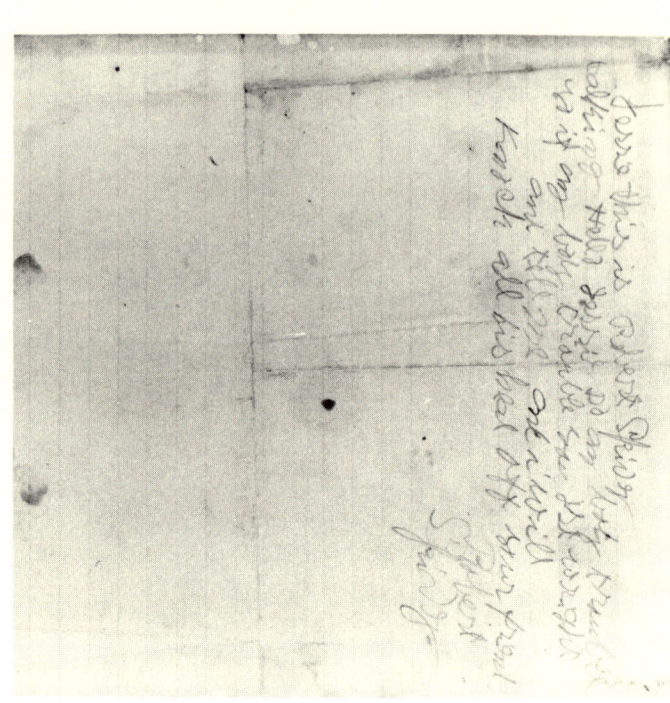

Kiss this is Robert Spivy talking Tell Bob do not be as if any body and I will know all about it Your friend

Robert Spivy

LETTER FROM ROBERT SPIVY ("RAB")
TO ELIZABETH ALLSTON PRINGLE, DECEMBER 16, 1908

From Allston-Pringle-Hill Collection

LETTER FROM JESSE SPIVY ("DAB")
TO JANE LOUISE ALLSTON HILL, FEBRUARY 20, 1906
From Allston-Pringle-Hill Collection

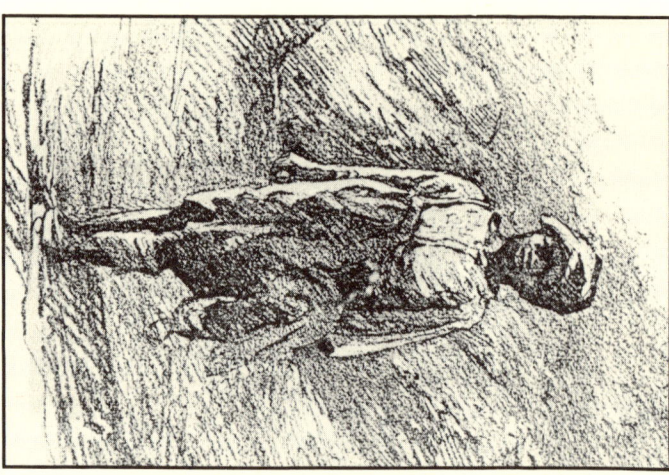

Drawing of "Dab"

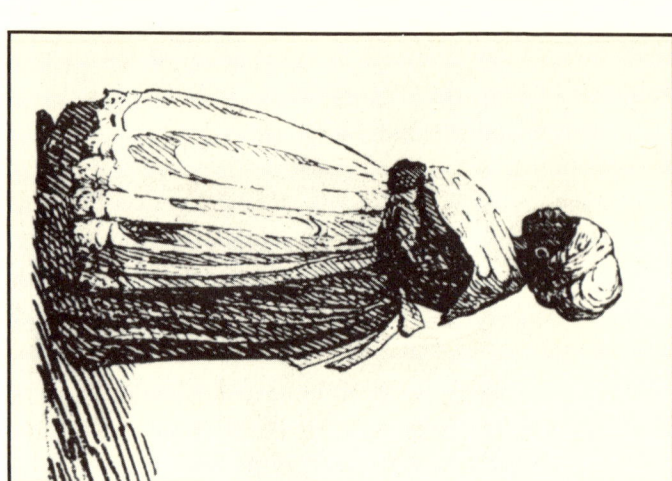

Drawing of "Chloe"

By Alice R. H. Smith
From *A Woman Rice Planter*, p. 249 and p. 338

ELIZABETH ALLSTON PRINGLE AT CHICORA WOOD

Reproduced from frontispiece of *Chronicles of Chicora Wood,* New York: Scribner, 1922; presumably her companion is Clarinda Lance ("Chloe")

Rab and Dab

CHAPTER I

1

Peaceville, Sept. 22. Went down to Casa Bianca to rouse the hands to action to-morrow, for we are to begin cutting Marshfield. I found the boy who blew himself up with gunpowder two days ago, in great suffering. Dressed his face and hands, using a feather to cover them with oil. He is a distressing object.

I gave orders that every man, woman, and child should be in the field early to-morrow, and promised to be down early myself.

Sept. 23. Just as I was getting into the wagon very early this morning, carrying linen rags and olive oil to dress Nero's burns, and lunch for myself, and a few pears and things to give the hands, I saw a pitiful little black figure standing at the foot of the steps. It was Jonadab, the little black pock-marked pygmy who has been coming all summer to beg for kitchen scraps, and old garments, and anything I would or could give. He stutters fearfully.

'What is it, Jonadab?' I asked; 'I am in a great hurry to-day, so you must talk quick.'

After what seemed to me a long time and many convulsions of his little frame, he shot out, 'Ma bery sick. 'E bad off, en 'e baig yu fuh cum.'

I told Jim to drive to his mother's house, which I knew was not far off in the pine woods, but just how far I did not know, for though I had sent things to her constantly, I had never been to her house myself.

The road was well-nigh impassable for the wagon, and Jim, being provoked at this interruption, drove very fast and, it seemed to me, recklessly. At last I said to him, 'Stop; and I will walk the rest of the way with Jonadab.' The pine forest shimmered and glittered in the slanting rays of the early morning sun. Every blade of grass was laden with dew diamonds, and the slippery, brown pine-needles were damp under my feet.

When I started on this diversion from my plans I was distinctly irritated at the delay caused by this extra drive of two miles. It seemed so all-important to me to get to Casa Bianca early; for with the hands I have, six acres is as much as I can get cut in one day, and there are twenty-six acres in the field. And this is such a stormy season of the year. But as I walked through the solemn pines with the little shriveled gnome ahead of me to show the path, I heard the voice of God in the sough of the pines, and a change came over my spirit. The sense of hurry and impatience left me.

Jonadab in a little while pointed through the pines, and I saw a little log cabin. In the doorway two atoms of black humanity were sitting very near together, and Jonadab volunteered the information that they were his little brother and his youngest sister. As they saw me they rose and disappeared into the house, and I followed.

There were two rooms. The first one had a very unsteady pine table, two chairs, and three pots in the fireplace. I passed through this to the inner room,

Chapter I

where on the floor lay a woman, terribly swollen, her eyes protruding from her head, her breath coming in quick, heavy sobs. She seemed unconscious. Two Negro women who had just come in stood beside her. One was her mother, with whom she had quarreled a year ago, and who had never come near her through her long months of suffering and illness, leaving her alone with her little children. But to-day, hearing from a neighbor that Abby was dying, she rushed in, too late to be of any use.

I knelt down on the dirty floor beside the sick woman, and tried to give her some milk and stimulant which I had brought. But her teeth were closed and refused to admit the spoon, and I realized that she was actually dying. Then I laid my hand on her clammy one, and bending low, I said, 'Abby, can you hear me?' There was no sign of comprehension or consciousness. I was very eager to make her hear, so I went on speaking very slowly and distinctly: 'I will take care of your two little boys and see that they never want. Do you understand? I will take Jonadab and Rechab myself, and care for them.' Then there was a slight quivering of the eyelids, a faint token of assent and satisfaction, before the stony stare of death returned.

I prayed aloud with all my soul for the spirit which was struggling to leave its poor earthly tenement; while the women moaned and swayed and ejaculated, 'Yes, Laud; do, Laud,' as the sentences of the prayer for the dying fell fervently on the still, hot air, and the groans of the dying woman were less loud. Then I sang,—

> 'Jesus, Lover of my soul,
> Let me to Thy bosom fly.'

The women and children joined with their high, clear voices, and while they sang, 'Cover my defenseless head with the shadow of thy wing,' the last painful breaths were drawn, and the immortal spirit took its flight and returned to God who gave it, and who is merciful and loving, and knows all the struggles, all the temptations, all the warping influences which had kept it from its highest possibilities.

I talked with Rachael, the mother, who, now that the poor daughter was gone, spoke of her with loud and hysterical affection. When I offered to take the children she said that she, the grandmother, was the person to take them; no one would do for them as she would and she could not think of giving them up to anybody. I was surprised, but pleased, at this her suddenly aroused maternal feeling, and acquiesced in it, saying, 'Very well, Rachael, I agree with you that you are the proper person to take care of the children, and that no one can do it as well. I will provide everything that the two boys need, their food and clothing; just let me know what they need.'

By this time the house was full of excited neighbors, lamenting and going on as though they had been active friends of the poor deceased. I promised to send what was needed for Abby's 'laying out.' They said the 'Chuch' would provide the coffin, and attend to the funeral, for she was 'Babtist member, in full standin', en belonged to de sassiety, en dey was boun' to bury um.'

Having done the little I could, I left the house of death, much exhausted and agitated, to return to the work-a-day world outside. I drove home and told Chloe to send one of my gowns and two sheets to Rachael at once; and then started on the twelve-mile drive to Casa Bianca.

When I got there I had my saddle put on Mollie, and

Chapter I

rode down the ricefield banks to Marshfield. There were the gayly dressed women, laughing, singing, talking, as they cut down the golden heads with great dexterity; laying them on the stubble so that the sun could dry them enough to tie to-morrow. The gay scene, which usually gave me so much pleasure, only saddened me now. The tragedy I had witnessed haunted me, and I wondered how in the eyes of the great Judge of all things my life would compare with that whose end I had seen.

I reproached myself bitterly for never having visited her before. I had sent her supplies: food, clothing, and so forth,—yes; but that was not all. If I had only gone to see her and talk with her, I should not now be filled with self-condemnation. God forgive me for not giving her my time. What are all my occupations in comparison with helping a human soul? My dear little niece went, I know, and read the Bible to her on Sunday afternoons, but I was always 'too busy' or 'too tired' to go. Woe is me!

And so the long, blazing summer day wore on—a day of penance—and the words of Good's wonderful poem, 'The Lady's Dream,' rang in my ears:—

> But Evil is wrought by want of thought,
> As well as want of heart.

2

The above extract from my diary shows how Rab and Dab first came into my life. During the autumn I kept in touch with them, seeing them daily. I sent them food and clothing, and tried to see if Rachael was doing full justice to them. She was an excellent cook, and had been employed in that capacity by some ladies in the village. But as soon as she took the children she gave up her place, saying that she could not attend to the children and her work; as the boys had two older sisters of twelve and fourteen, this was evidently not the real reason.

Abby had been so helpless in her ill health with her large family, that some of the gentlemen of the neighborhood had secured for her a monthly allowance from the county, and though I had told Rachael I would see that this was continued for the children, five in number, she feared that her having a place as cook, and consequently being self-supporting might prevent it, so she gave up her situation and lived on the provisions allowed the children, with the result that the little ones looked hungry and continued their stealing. The whole family had learned from infancy to go into the fields within their reach and grabble potatoes, to gather unripe corn for roasting ears, to catch every chicken and steal all the eggs which were not under lock and key. The two elder girls had been taken up, tried, and found guilty of theft before the poor mother's death. Their only punishment had been to be kept in confinement until the crops were harvested.

This rich lowland rice-planting region would be a paradise if people could live on their plantations all the year round; but the Anglo-Saxon has always been susceptible to malarial fever, and in the early settlement of the country suffered much from it. After some years they found that by leaving their beautiful homes on the rivers with their luxuriant tropical growth during the hot months, and living in the belt of pine forest (which is generally found a few miles inland from the rivers), they secured perfect health. With this knowledge the planters joined in selecting some high, sandy, well-

Chapter I

drained spot in the original forest, and built lodges with big rooms and wide piazzas in large shady yards, and at the end of May they moved their families from the plantation and remained in the health-giving pines until the first heavy frost in November, when the little villages, so gay and populous all summer, were left silent and deserted during the winter. Peaceville is one of these hamlets of refuge from mosquitoes and malaria, and is only four miles from my plantation and winter home, Cherokee, and here I spend the hot months, driving back to the ricefields every day to look after the work.

This year, when I left Peaceville early in November, I established the orphans and their grandmother in one of the outbuildings in my yard, as it was much more comfortable than the little log hut in the woods. After the move I tried to see them at least once a week. I soon saw a change for the worse: they got thinner and thinner, with swollen faces and large stomachs like the famine pictures from India I was seeing in the illustrated papers.

One bitter cold day in January, Elihu, who is the blackest of my retainers, being of such a rich shade that his mother always spoke of him as 'dat black nigger,' a man whom I have helped out of every variety of trouble, and who has a feeble desire to help me in return, if it can be done with no effort beyond speech, came to tell me that he heard that Rachael was going to move to Gregory, the county seat, eighteen miles away, on that day. In spite of the cold, I ordered the buckboard at once and drove out to see Rachael. I found the house in great confusion,—bedding tied up in huge bundles, boxes and trunks corded, and Rachael in her Sunday best.

'Why, Rachael, where are you going this cold morning?'

'Well, ma'am, I'm goin' to move to town. I got chillun dere to help me.'

'I think that is a great mistake, Rachael. Here you have no house rent, you have all the wood you can burn without paying a cent, and your daughter lives very near you. If your sons are willing to help you, let them send you what they can spare; it will go much further here.'

But Rachael had made up her mind and was not to be dissuaded. She was tired of the country, and was going to move to town. She had hired an ox-wagon to take her to the river, where she would take the steamer.

When I had tried every argument without avail, I said, 'Then I will take the boys with me. I am not willing for them to starve or spend their time in jail for stealing.' Turning to the children, crouching over the fire, I said, 'Jonadab, do you want to go with me?'

He, after many convulsions, shot out, 'Yes, 'um.'

Rechab was inside the huge fireplace behind the logs, squatting down; an extraordinary-looking black shrimp.

'Rab, do you want to go with me?'

Rab's little black face was stolid and expressionless like some little old man's. It was some time before he could be made to understand the situation, but when at last his grandmother pulled him out of the chimney, and cuffing him, said, 'Speak up, boy, speak up,' he grunted out, 'Um,' and nodded his head violently.

Then I told Rachael that she must sign a paper giving up all claim to the children, to which she responded vociferously, ''Tain' no nuse for me to sign a paper,

Miss Pashuns. You'se welcome to the chillun. I'se heartily tired of dem; dey's jes' nachully bad chillun; deys tek after dey pa, what was a furrin man, en corrupted my daughter. You kin tek 'em en welcome.'

Then the women assembled in the room to see Rachael's departure, began to exclaim, 'My law, Aun' Rachael, dem chillun sho' is lucky. Miss Pashuns 'ull do de bes' for dem po' mudderless ting'; and so on.

I called for the last shirts I had made the children, but these could not be found. Whether they were so securely packed up as to be out of reach, or whether Rachael had sold them, I never knew, for I lost patience and took the boys out to the buckboard in their rags. There my dainty little niece Aline, who was waiting for me, was filled with dismay at sight of them, and exclaimed, 'Aunt Patience, you are not going to take them *now,* with us?'

'Yes, they are coming *now with us,*' I answered, in a voice of such determination that Aline said no more.

In the back of the buckboard, fortunately, there were some tow-sacks which I was taking home. I had the boys climb into the buckboard, covered them with the sacks, and drove off rapidly. In a little while a small voice made itself heard from behind: 'I cold.' I put Rab into one of the sacks, tied it round his neck securely, covered him with the others, and drove on.

3

I shall never forget the consternation which took possession of the yard when I reached home. Jim, my good man-of-all-work, said nothing when I told him to help the children out and release Rab from the sack;

but as I led the two forlorn mites through the yard to the old wash-house, where there were two rooms, one occupied by Goody, the cook, I was aware of very black looks on all sides.

I did not appear, however, to see them, but said to the cook, 'Goody, I put these children in this room next to you, and I beg you to give an eye to them. I will not ask you to do anything for them, for I will look after them myself as much as possible, only at night give an ear to them.'

Goody, who was a very short, plump little figure, neat and tidy but very ugly, drew herself up to her full height, about four feet six inches, and said, 'Miss Pashuns, dem chillun is too duhty for lib in de room nex' me.'

'Yes, Goody, I know they are terribly dirty, but we are going to try and make them different. You know the Good Father promises a special blessing to those who help the orphan, and I feel sure you will wish to get some of that blessing.'

Then I promptly left, having put the children on a bench by the fireplace, where I had Jim, on whose help I can always count, make a fire.

And then Aline and I rushed upstairs, and soon the sewing-machine was in rapid operation. That day we cut and made a suit apiece for the waifs, so that when I had them scrubbed that night their old clothes could be burned. Besides this we made a mattress to fill with nice, clean straw for their bed, and got blankets and comforts for their bedding.

When I called on Chloe to find the blankets I could best spare from the house, her aspect was truly appalling. Chloe had been the comfort of my life for years, having made it possible, by her devotion and faithfulness, for me to live in the old home alone since my mother's death, with no white person within a mile or two; so that she had been a friend as well as servant. This terrible innovation, however, was almost more than Chloe could bear with respectful equanimity. She looked so stolid and unsympathetic that I felt obliged to make a little speech somewhat like that I had made to Goody, about the blessing promised to those who care for the orphan, but Chloe answered with great dignity, 'Miss Pashuns, of course I'm only a sarvant, en of course you know better en me, but I tink 't is a bery dangrus ting to harber furriners in yo' ya'd, en moreober, chillun ob a teefin' fambly. I would n't say a wud if dey was we own people orphan, but I kyant undertek to tek keer ob no furrin chillun.'

There was a distinct note of rebellion in this speech, and I answered promptly, 'I have not asked you to take care of them, Chloe. I will do that. But I thought you would wish to share the promised blessing. I see, however, that you do not realize what a serious thing it is to reject a blessing.'

And passing on to the sewing-room, I worked with enthusiasm, stopping reluctantly for dinner, and by sundown everything was finished.

Then we formed a procession: Jim ahead with a huge kettle of hot water, then Chloe with soap and towels, and Aline and I behind. The tub had already been put by the fire in the orphans' room. They were washed and scrubbed thoroughly with hot water and carbolic soap, their new nighties put on, and their old clothes burned. After this was done, and the tub was removed, I had them kneel down and say the dear little child's prayer which has helped so many children through so many dark nights:—

> Jesus, tender Shepherd, hear me,
> Bless thy little lamb to-night,
> Through the darkness be Thou near me,
> Keep me safe till morning light.

Then they got into their nice clean bed, and we left them.

It took Aline and me days of hard sewing to complete the boys' new outfit. Neither of us was accustomed to make boys' clothes, and the want of patterns worried us a good deal; and then the number of buttonholes seemed alarming; but we invented some patterns not requiring so many.

The second day after their arrival Chloe came in and said, 'Miss Pashuns, you got to be bery pertickler how you feed dese chillun. Ef you give dem much as dey want you'll kill dem sho.'

'Very well, Chloe, use your discretion about it. I leave their feeding to you.'

'Yes, ma'am, cause dey is mos' starved, en dey kyant satisfy. I give dem dey dinner, and befo' I start wid mine dey done dem own, and den dey look at mine so pitiful I 'bleege to give 'em mo', but Jim say 't is dangrus to feed 'em too much.'

Jim told me that when he was eating his dinner one day, Rab, having finished his own, watched him with such greedy eyes that he said, 'Rechab, you ain't had enuff?'

Rab answered, 'No sah, I neber had me belly full in me life.'

'Well, Rab, we'll stall you. Dat's what we'll hab to do, Chloe. Dey's been here ten days, and dere's no danger now. We'll stall dem.'

Chloe agreed, so the next day the plan was carried

Chapter I

out. More dinner was cooked than usual, and the boys were given plate after plate until they said they had had enough, and then Jim and Chloe felt that they had accomplished a feat, and assured me that there would never in future be any trouble in satisfying them. I only heard of this after it was over, for I would have forbidden it as dangerous, never having heard of such a thing.

I gave the elder, Dab, a little axe, and told him he could get the fallen branches of the oaks which covered the park in front of the house, and carry them to the kitchen for the stove. This he did with delight, bringing them in a cart made of a box on wooden wheels, Rab always trotting behind; and after a while they lost their stolid look.

It was a great relief to me to find that Chloe was thawing toward the outcasts. Jim was always good to them and gave all the help he could, for Jim had a boy of his own about the size of Jonadab and his heart was tender to them.

It was not long before Goody announced that she was going: she could not stand those dirty children in the room next to her. I was greatly shocked at this. She had been with me a long time, and was an excellent cook, clean, cheerful, honest, and willing until the arrival of the orphans. I talked with her, and told her they were already improving, and soon would be quite different. There was no use. Go she would. Her dignity was injured as well as her feelings. It was a great loss to me. She not only cooked, but looked after the poultry, and besides I had grown fond of the little old woman.

Now Chloe had to cook and she was a splendid

cook; but she had left the kitchen on account of ill health, and I feared another breakdown if she undertook the cooking as well as the maid's work.

However, she was eager to do it, and I looked out for some one to take care of the poultry. Bonaparte told me that he heard Cinthy was at a neighboring plantation, very poor, and he thought I might get her, and as he said it would be a great help to her I told him to get her. So Cinthy came and took possession of the room Goody had left, next to the children. She was only middle-aged, but she seemed very helpless and a little cracked. She was to get three dollars a month and her food. She had been very friendless and poor, and being what Chloe calls a 'Maus nigger,' which means she had belonged to the same master, she was acceptable to the other servants. She was perfectly delighted to get the place, and never met me in the yard without making a deep courtesy, clasping her hands and looking up to heaven and making known her joy. 'Ain't yo' see, my Maussa always *did* tek keer of him people, en now 'e gone, but 'e ain't furgit me. 'E sen' 'e chile for find me, en bring me home en tek keer of me. Yes, 'e send 'e chile for mind me.'

Her light work was well done, and she was good to the children, and they were beginning to look happy, to my great satisfaction. One night when I went to hear their prayers Aline heard them singing, and motioned to me not to make a noise. The door was ajar, and we looked in. The two little boys were sitting on their wooden stools in front of a very bright lightwood fire, staring into it, swaying back and forth in time to the rhythm of the strange little hymn they were singing.[1]

[1] See page 18.

Chapter I

It seemed to me wonderful that these little children, who appeared to be about six and four years old, should remember words and tune so well.

Every Sunday afternoon I taught them a very easy little form of catechism used for very young children. When I asked Jonadab the first question, 'Who made you?' with violent contortions he shot out, 'My ma.'

'Yes,' I explained, 'but God made your mother, and you and everything else in the world.'

The next question is, 'What did He make you for?'

Again Dab shot out a prompt answer, 'Fo' work.'

The answer in the little book is, 'For his glory.' I was puzzled how to combine the two ideas to reach his comprehension. *Laborare est orare,* and this little black mortal could only glorify his Maker by doing with all his heart his very small duties.

After this I gave up using the regular catechism, and told them the wonderful story of the Creation and Redemption of the world in my own words, and they soon learned to tell it themselves with dramatic effect. That story of the whole garden being at the disposal of Adam and Eve, except the one tree whose fruit they were forbidden to touch, appealed strongly to their understanding, and when they told of the temptation they always said, 'Satan tu'n 'eself into a black snake, en 'e crawl up to Eve, en 'e say, "Eat um, 'e good, en 'e'll mek yo' wise," en den Eve eat um.'

I always allowed them to tell it to me in their own way, and being well acquainted with the black snake, they preferred it to the word serpent. I then taught them a simple hymn which they seemed to find very difficult, and then I let them sing one of their own little hymns, 'sperituals,' the nigs called them; and in this way I heard all they knew, and going at once to the piano, I tried to write them down in the keys in which the waifs sang them.

4

As soon as I had an opportunity I bought each of them a suit of 'store clothes.' I got them for four and six years, but they were a little large. Still, the boys gloried in them and wore them on Sundays.

Their joy was to take the little axe and cut and bring in load after load of the small dead limbs which make splendid hot fires, and they won their way into Chloe's heart by keeping the kitchen woodbox full. By the spring they had become very merry, and the change in

Chapter I

them from stolid indifference to intelligent interest in everything, gave me great pleasure.

There was one great trouble and distress as they grew happy and at home. The propensities I had hoped would disappear entirely with sufficient food and clothing began to peep out. Not an egg could ever be got for the house. The boys watched the hens and knew their nests; and they stole out early in the morning before any one was awake, took all the eggs into their room, ate some, hid some, and sold some to any one and for anything. Chloe's utmost vigilance could not come up with them.

The second spring they were with us, Chloe had raised a number of broods of beautiful chickens to the size of partridges. Then they began to disappear rapidly. I said to Chloe, 'I fear it is our cat.' Chloe answered, ''T is varmint, Miss Pashuns. Ef it was de cat I would see um for sartain, kase I'se very watchful. But you kyant ketch varmint. Dey favors de daak.'

One evening Chloe had been to the garden about an eighth of a mile from the house to pick green peas. She had left Rab in charge of the yard, and she suddenly remembered that she had not locked her room door, so she returned earlier than was her wont. As she approached she saw Rab sitting on the kitchen steps where she had told him to stay, and her heart glowed as she said to herself, 'Rechab is sholy gettin' to be a sma't boy to tek keer of de ya'd so good.' He was shelling an ear of corn and the great crowds of little Plymouth Rocks were running over the steps and his knees, eager to get the corn as it fell.

Chloe's heart stopped beating, for suddenly Rab made a dive, caught a chicken, seized it by the feet, swung it round rapidly, then cracked its neck with his teeth, and stuffed it into the bosom of his shirt. Chloe rushed forward and seized him. Having caught him thus red-handed, she shook him and screamed, 'You wicked boy, I seen yo' kill dat chicken.'

Rab tried to escape, but she held him, and made him take the little warm body from his shirt.

'Aint yo' shame to ac' so awful, Rab? I trus' yo', and lef' yo' in charge of the ya'd, en I ketch yo' en see yo' wid my own eye crack dat checken neck wid yo' wicked teeth. Ain't yo' feared the debbil 'll come for yo' dis minit en carry yo'm straight to hell? I feel um a-comin'. Tell me de trufe befor' 'e get yo', boy. I don't want yo' for bu'n.'

Thus exhorted and adjured, terror seized Rab, and he cried, 'Aun' Chloe, don' let de debbil ketch me, en I'll tell yo' all. I done kill twenty. I eat some, en I hide some under de grape-harbor, en I'll sho' yo' de place ef yo'll save me from de debbil.'

He took her under the grape-arbor and to several places where he had the bodies hid.

When Chloe told me, I was wretched, and my first thought was that she did not give the child enough to eat. But when I suggested this, Chloe was indignant, and said in an unnecessarily loud tone of voice that Jonadab and Rechab ate more than Jim and Ben the field hand and herself put together. 'An' as fo' yo', Miss Pashuns, Rechab eat mo' in one day than yo' eat in a week. Meat, en rice, en turnip, en greens, en tetta, en molasses, not to say all de aig, so dat I kyant so much as gi' yo' a biled aig fo' yo' breakfast. No, ma'am, Miss Pashuns, don' 'cuse me o' not feedin' dat chile, fo' I does stuff 'im. Lessen yo' 'lows me to give 'im a good licken, Satan's boun' to carry dat chile off bodily.'

Chapter I

Up to this time I had insisted on moral suasion as the right method of dealing with the boys. In their old life they had been accustomed to beating and harsh words, and I wanted them to have a change in their experiences, and so I had shamed them for bad conduct and rewarded them for good conduct. Now, however, justice and Chloe demanded severity. Rechab had to suffer in his little black body for the evil deeds thereof, so I authorized Chloe to execute what she considered suitable punishment, knowing I could trust to her tender heart not to be too severe.

Chloe's method of administering the rod was unique. 'Now, Rab,' she said, 'I goin' to bag yo' befo' I lick yo'.'

Rab cried aloud for mercy, but she was firm, and put a sack over the culprit's head and tied it round his waist, and then proceeded with much noise and flourish to lay on a light switch. Rechab, however, made a great outcry, and promised volubly never to do so any more; and certainly for a while he abstained from chicken slaughter.

5

That November I had gone to the State Fair and committed a great extravagance. I had bought a pair of beautiful white turkeys from the Vanderbilt farm at Biltmore. They cost what seemed an enormous price, but they were said to be hardy and to have a very domestic and contented turn of mind, never wandering far from home.

My great difficulty in raising turkeys had been their roaming propensities. They would wander off to a distance and get caught by foxes and other varmints. But I had high hopes of raising a great many with this new variety. One day in May the poultry yard was in great excitement. Mrs. Vander had been sitting on twenty-five eggs for a month, and they were expected to hatch. Mr. Vander, who weighed forty pounds, strutted about in great pride.

When Chloe went to feed Mrs. V. that evening, she found twenty-four beauties in the nest. Her joy and pride were almost equal to Mr. V.'s. The little turkeys—pee-pees, as Chloe called them—were only two weeks old when the time came to move to the pine land for the summer, so the dear little roly-poly yellow things were put in a basket and taken out tenderly in the buckboard, while Mrs. V. was made comfortable in a small coop and followed with the other poultry in the wagon.

I had had a new house built for the distinguished family, all wired so that no harm could befall them, and yet they would have plenty of fresh air, and they were very happy when they found themselves together in such delightful quarters after the trials of the move.

As soon as we had settled down after the move I sent Jonadab to school, there being one in the little pine-land hamlet of Peaceville, under the auspices of the church, and kept by two ladies, mother and daughter. They were charming women, the mother still beautiful, showing her Greek descent in her perfect features and exquisite skin; both so refined, so thorough and conscientious,—they certainly were as near saints as mortal women ever get to be. She had been an heiress, and had married a wealthy rice-planter, but had been left after the war with nothing but her land, of which she could make no use without money to pay for labor. No one will ever know what privations she went through with her children after her husband's death, for she never made any moan, and brought up her children to do without, smilingly. What a power it gives when one has learned to do without!

For twenty-five cents a month for each child they gave up their whole time and strength to guiding the little dusky minds in the path of learning. They returned the quarter Jonadab carried, saying it would give them pleasure to teach him without pay, and his days of joy began.

At an early hour every morning, in a blue denim suit with a spotless white shirt, and his blue denim schoolbag on his shoulder, he traveled to school, a broad grin on his black face. I had feared that the strange hesitation and convulsion of his speech would make him a very trying pupil, but the good ladies sent excellent reports of him. He was very attentive and docile, and learned quickly.

I thought Rechab was too young and mischievous to go to school, and so he made things lively at home. As soon as Jonadab returned and sat down to study his lessons, Rab sat beside him, and Dab taught him the spelling orally, so that Rab could spell apparently just as well as Dab, only he knew not a single letter.

During the summer I went to the mountains to visit a sister, and things went on very satisfactorily. I had Jim write me a weekly letter telling all that went on at the plantation and in the yard, and he reported everything as serene until the autumn, when Chloe announced in a letter the death of Mr. Vander and the disappearance of all the little V.'s, and in a delicate way hinted that their death had not been a natural one, but accused no one.

I knew from the mysterious tone of the letter that something was very wrong, and when I got home the tale was told. Rechab had chased and killed Mr. Vander, and caught the little ones and either eaten or sold them. Mrs. Vander had been wounded, but Chloe had nursed her back to health. It was a sad outcome of my experiment in improved stock, and I was at a loss what to do, but finally I concluded to appear ignorant of Rab's evil deeds during my absence.

The boys were quite well and much grown. They seemed delighted to see me back, as were all the servants and the Negroes on the plantation.

The first week in November the move from the pine land back to the river, that *bête noire* of life on a rice-plantation, was accomplished. Cinthy, who had been left in the yard alone during the summer, was overjoyed to see the return of the household. She had the yard raked very clean, no weeds, no dead leaves anywhere; so I presented her with a calico frock and a new pair of shoes, and her cup of joy seemed overflowing. I wanted her to try on the shoes at once so that if they did not fit I could exchange them. I had got the number she told me she wore,—threes; but the vanity of giving a number which is entirely too small is very common among the Negroes, and I wanted to see for myself if these fitted.

But Cinthy refused to try them on, saying, 'To-night I gwine wash me foot, en I'll try de sho' on to-morrow when me foot clean.'

The next morning as I sat at the breakfast-table, Chloe came in to say that Cinthy did not 'feel so well.'

I was much surprised, for she had seemed so well and so gay the day before.

'Is she in bed, Chloe?' I asked.

Chapter I

'Oh, no, ma'am, I lef' um de sit by de fire, but 'e say 'e ain't feel so good.'

I poured out and sweetened heavily a cup of coffee and took it out at once to Cinthy's room. I knocked, but getting no answer pushed the door open and went in. Cinthy was saying her prayers, kneeling by the bed; so I sat down on the little bench by the fire, and set the cup of coffee on the hearth.

After a few minutes, thinking she had fallen asleep, I went to her and laid my hand gently on her shoulder. To my horror, the whole figure shook just as though I had touched a doll. Cinthy was dead! It was a dreadful shock. By her side were the new shoes yet untried. The bed was tidily made up, the room swept, and everything around was neat and commonplace, but the mighty dignity of Death had entered the poor room, and there was a great pathos in the solemn figure. She had sunk on her knees to hear the Master's summons. Simple, unlearned Cinthy had been called up higher. She knew the great secret of the hereafter.

I called Chloe, who almost fainted when I told her. I called Bonaparte, my head man and carpenter, and sent Jim for the doctor; but there was nothing to be done. It was heart disease of which no one had any suspicion. I sent down to Cinthy's son, who lived in Gregory, and her friends were notified and they assembled promptly and sang 'sperituals' and recounted Cinthy's virtues, which they all seemed now to appreciate.

The son, who owned his house and lot in town, a horse and buggy and pair of oxen, had never thought of providing his mother with the smallest comfort while she lived. Now, however, he paid her his tribute of tears. I had Bonaparte make a coffin, buying all the necessary things at the neighboring country store; and as I could get nothing that looked nice for the inside, I took my work-basket out under an oak tree, and pinked out yards and yards of white trimming, which was greatly admired. I cut a deep scallop, and then a cluster of holes in it, which gave a very fine effect.

It was a relief to sit out under the canopy of Heaven and have this mechanical occupation while I recovered from the shock and agitation. I had given Chloe a nice outfit from my own things for the 'laying-out,' and a large bow of black ribbon for Cinthy's neck. All of these little adornments of the empty shell mean so much to Negroes, and I knew I could in no other way do as much for the limited faithful creature.

The simple funeral took place the next day with much circumstance, and its wild minor music, so descriptive of death as a terror, brought to my memory the many nights when as a child I had covered my head with the bed clothing to keep from my ears that heartbreaking wail; and even now, as the last rites were being paid to Cinthy in the burying-ground they all love so well, some of the same feeling crept upon me, and it was hard to realize that 'Death is swallowed up in Victory,' that it is truly only the Gate to Life.

Beside her parents and grandparents Cinthy was laid to rest. Then came the disposal of her 'ting.' The son said, magnanimously, that he wanted nothing, so Chloe proceeded to distribute the little treasures among the few friends who had been kind to Cinthy when she was in need, before I found her, and 'brought her home,' as she always said. It was very little,—a cooking pot, a spider, a tub, her bedding, and clothing, including the new calico dress; but they were much prized by the recipients. No one wanted her little bed-

Chapter I

stead, a neat little home-made frame; but Cinthy thought a great deal of it for it was made of 'Indian Pride,' she said. I had this put out in the orchard, and the untried shoes I took back to the house.

I told Jim he must take the boys to sleep in his house for a while till the sense of emptiness in the next room had passed away; so he invited them; but Jonadab refused, saying they did not want to leave their room; and they slept next to the empty room without one thought of fear, and after a month begged me to let them move into Cinthy's room, which had been scoured and whitewashed. I consented, and they moved in and seemed delighted with their new quarters.

During this winter Jonadab continued to go to school, though it gave him a walk of eight miles and I thought it was too far for such a little fellow. He was anxious to go, however, and insisted that it was not too far, and proved that he was right by growing in health and strength all winter. He brought my mail with him every day from the post-office, which was just opposite his schoolhouse in Peaceville. He had a hoop from a barrel which he rolled along the level road, and made the distance in very short time, and apparently without fatigue. Rab wanted to go too, but I would not consent, and he spent his time getting 'bresh' with the little axe and the little cart. He still indulged his great fondness for eggs, but was willing to divide now, and brought some to the house.

CHAPTER II

1

THE second summer after the transplanting of the orphans found them growing in favor with every one. Really Chloe was becoming proud of them. When Jonadab started to school every morning, in his dark blue denim suit, he was pleasing to the eye, he was so shiningly clean with his startlingly white teeth. As soon as he got back from school, he studied his lessons, had his dinner, and then, with the little axe and the wheelbarrow, followed by Rechab with the hatchet and little cart, which Dab now looked down upon as a plaything, he went out into the woods and cut a good supply for the kitchen, never waiting to be told. Chopping wood was his favorite relaxation, as it was that of Mr. Gladstone; and so long as he had this safety valve for his superfluous energy he could keep out of mischief.

Rab got into endless trouble in the long summer mornings while Dab was at school. One day I was sewing in the parlor, with the thick board shutters nearly closed, to keep out the heat, when I heard a shrill woman's voice, raised in angry abuse in the yard. I listened attentively but all I could distinguish was, 'I'll beat dat limb o' Satan, sho's you bawn.'

I went out on the back porch and saw in the yard a tall brown woman working herself into a fury. She held in one hand a big stick, and led, or rather dragged, a small boy with the other,—he screaming aloud to add to the clamor.

'What is the matter?' I repeated several times before I could make myself heard.

Then her shrill angry voice rose to a shriek, and I could only hear Rab's name coupled with that of the Prince of Darkness.

At last I said, 'I cannot possibly listen to such language; if you speak properly, in a moderate voice, I will hear what you have to say; otherwise I will go in.'

The woman quieted down then and told her story.

'I sen' dis chile, Ben, to de sto' wid t'ree cent fu' buy salt, en dis yah black wicked boy meet um ne path, en fight um, en tek de money, en I gwine bruk eb'ry bone in 'e body.' And she waved the big stick.

I was greatly distressed at this highway robbery on Rab's part and I said to the woman, 'I am shocked beyond measure at what you tell me, and though I cannot allow you to beat Rechab, I promise that I will have him severely punished. Here are the three cents he took; indeed, here are five cents which were to have been Rechab's on Saturday if he had been good. He has entirely forfeited them, and he must pay them to you'; and I placed the five coppers in Rab's hand and made him give them to the woman, who went off more than satisfied at this unexpected good luck.

As soon as she had gone, I called Ancrum, the old

Chapter II

man whom I had employed cutting down underbrush and trimming up trees in the grounds. He was a most respectable old darkey, who did faithfully and thoroughly everything that was given him to do, and bore a high character for honesty and industry; and though he was nearly eighty he was a strong, able-bodied man. When he came I said, 'Daddy Ancrum, would you mind giving little Rechab a good whipping for me?'

'Not at all, my missis, I'll do um wid pledger.'

'Now, Daddy Ancrum, I do not want you to beat him, but he must be well punished, for he met a boy smaller than himself on the road, fought him and took his money from him, and if he is not punished, he will end his days in the penitentiary, if not on the gallows.'

Daddy Ancrum went off to cut a good switch. He took quite a time, as he wanted to find a hickory; and while he was gone I used all my powers of speech on Rab, trying to make him see the wickedness of his action, and brought him at last to confess his guilt,— which he had stolidly denied at first,—and even to tell what he had done with the money. He had bought three sticks of mint candy at the store. When Daddy Ancrum came for him he was penitent. I told Ancrum to take Rab some distance out in his own beloved woods, so that the little village would not be disturbed too much, for I knew Rab's voice would wake the echoes in the tall pines. Again I charged the old man not to be too severe. I did this without Rab's hearing me.

Ancrum answered, 'Miss Pashuns, you need n't fret. I had twelve chillun en I know how fu' *lick* chillun widout *beat* um.'

I went into the sitting-room and closed it up as much as possible and took up my sewing again. In spite of my efforts not to hear, however, I was much agitated by Rab's yells; it sounded really as though he were being killed, and I was debating whether I should not send Chloe out to say that was enough, when there was a change, a sudden cessation of the shrieks, and, instead, a fierce barking of dogs and Rechab's voice raised loud in command. I rushed out to see what had happened. The three dogs, Rag, Tag, and Bobtail, were devoted to Rab, and hearing his cries of distress, they had rushed to the rescue and attacked the executioner with such ferocity that Rab had to keep them off, and actually had to use the rod which he had been feeling, to prevent their biting the old man. Needless to say the punishment ended therewith, Rechab, as usual, in the ascendant, and much elated by his position of controller of the dogs. I must say I felt proud that Rechab had used all his strength to keep the dogs from biting Daddy Ancrum. A mean nature would have rejoiced in seeing him bitten, instead of doing all he could to protect him.

The solemnity of the preparations, and, no doubt, the solidity of the few strokes given, impressed Rab very sensibly, and for a few weeks after that he was alarmingly good. I had the hickory hung up on the back porch as a reminder.

During this interlude of perfection Rechab devoted himself to Chloe: he brought immense bundles of fagots for the kitchen stove, scoured the pantry, and caused Chloe great anxiety by his zeal in drawing water; the well was deep, the bucket heavy, and the curb low, and there was always a moment when it was uncertain whether the bucket would come up or Rab would go down. I felt that sooner or later he would join

Chapter II

Truth at the bottom of the well, and most uncongenial companions they would prove.

It was during this period of calm that Rab told Chloe, as he sat by her on the kitchen steps, that when he was a man and made plenty of money he would give her a big silver dollar for her own, and he would give 'Miss Pashuns a half dollar.'

When I made the boys their summer outfit, I made the usual blue denim trousers and jacket, but I put bands of red on some of the little shirts and bands of blue on others, which gave the boys great pleasure; and I thought it would make the washerwoman respect the clothes more and take more pains in washing them, for they were really very pretty and I liked to see the bright colors. Altogether this was a time of respite and happiness; and even Chloe went so far as to say to me, 'I declar', Miss Pashuns, dese chillun is great company an' great sarvis.'

2

About this time I was called away by illness in the family, and I left with a comfortable feeling that the boys had passed their worst stage and were now on the upward path. A great misfortune had befallen our little community. Miss Beth and her lovely mother had moved away. The school had passed into other hands, however, and Jonadab seemed to get on pretty well, and I left home with a quiet mind, telling Jim to write me a letter for himself one week, and for Chloe the next. Though he did all the writing, their letters were as different as possible, as he wrote down exactly what Chloe said and her letters were much more interesting than his; and in this way I heard everything, having the two points of view.

The first two letters reported everything as serene and satisfactory. Then came a mysterious letter from Chloe: she did not want to make me anxious, but the boys were not as good as they had been. She did not state anything definite. At last a letter showing great excitement came. Miss Somerville, the teacher, had gone to see Chloe to ask if Jonadab had been sick, for he had not been at school for two weeks.

This was a great blow to Chloe, for she had, she said, started him off at eight o'clock every morning with his bag of books, and the school-house was in sight from the front gate. She began investigating and found that he went past the school every day and waited in the woods until he knew Jim and herself had gone to the plantation four miles away, where Jim ran the cultivator in the corn and she tended the vegetable garden. As soon as Jonadab felt sure they had driven far enough away, he returned to the yard with a few kindred spirits and joined Rechab, who was left with the dogs, Rag, Tag and Bobtail, and a large supply of lunch.

Chloe did not go on to say in the letter how they occupied themselves, but asked me to write and tell her what she must do about Jonadab and the school. I wrote back at once and told Jim to give Jonadab a good switching and take him back to school, and to write me of the result. As soon as the distance would allow I heard from Jim; he had followed my directions but Jonadab would not go to school; he simply spent the days in the woods. I then wrote a solemn letter to Jonadab telling him that I was shocked and distressed at his conduct, that I had expected better things of

Chapter II

him, that I had given him the opportunity to learn, which was all I could do; that, as he would not go to school and learn his lessons, he must now learn to work, and that he must go with Jim to the plantation every day and work in the garden, and his books must be locked up until I got home; and I wrote to Jim to see that he did work.

After this the letters from Jim and Chloe showed great reticence and I was thankful to be spared the knowledge of anything going wrong at home, for after nursing my niece through an illness and back to health, I broke down completely and was threatened with nervous prostration, and had to remain in Asheville till the middle of October. When I did come home, instead of writing to have the wagon sent for me as usual, I got a vehicle in Gregory and drove up to the plantation, Cherokee.

Chloe and the boys were delighted to see me. I walked all around the garden and complimented them on the fine crops of turnips they had raised; then I ordered the wagon to drive out to Peaceville. Chloe called Jonadab and said, 'Bring up de pee-pee.'

In a few minutes Dab appeared driving before him five half-grown turkeys.

'These are very fine turkeys, Chloe,' I said, 'but where are the rest? I left twenty.'

'Dis is all dat's left, Miss Pashuns.'

So solemn was her tone that I forbore to ask questions.

Chloe fed the turkeys some cracked corn and then said, 'Bring de coob, Jonadab.'

Dab brought forward a small and very rough wooden coop.

'Put een de pee-pee,' ordered Chloe.

I watched with wonder, but did not interrupt what seemed to be a drill. With wonderful docility the little turkeys stepped leisurely into the coop, as Dab drummed on it with his fingers, having first scattered corn over the floor.

'Now fetch de wheel-barrer.' This was done. 'Rechab, help Jonadab put de coob een de wheel-barrer.' This was also done. Then came the final orders. 'Now, Jonadab, you sta't fu' de village, en don't you stop ne path to pass de time o' day. Rechab an' me'll ketch you ef you do.'

Thus adjured, Jonadab seized the handles and trotted off with the wheelbarrow at a brisk pace.

I did not speak until he was out of hearing, Rab having gone to open the gate for the equipage; then I asked, 'What is the meaning of this, Chloe? What are you going to do with the turkeys?'

'Miss Pashuns, I don't wan' ter cast yu down, jes' es yu get home, but I had to do dis way to save dese peepee fo' yu. I'll tell you all about it to-morrer.'

I said, 'Very well,' and by this time the wagon was ready and I got in, and told Chloe to get in with Rab by the driver. Before we had gone far we saw Jonadab ahead, trotting gayly with his remarkable turnout. When we caught up with him, which he tried his best to prevent, Rab asked me to let him get out and run along with Jonadab, which I allowed him to do.

As soon as he was out Chloe said, 'Well den, Miss Pashuns, yu'll hab to drive slow, sence yu let Rab git out, fo' ef yu let dem git out o' sight, dat's de las' o' dem pee-pee.'

The boys were in such high spirits, and made such good time, that only once or twice did I have to tell Jim to drive slowly. When we reached the pine-land house,

Chapter II 37

I was thankful to rest in the hammock swung on the broad piazza, and to feel the joy of getting home, even when there were only darkies and dogs to welcome me. Chloe got very quickly a nice savory supper for me, and the boys expended themselves in offering me fresh water drawn by them from the well, which they assured me was 'cool as ice.'

3

The next morning after breakfast Chloe sent the boys out to get wood and then appeared in the sitting-room in a glistening white apron and head-handkerchief and, dropping a curtsy, began.

'Now, Miss Pashuns, ef yu feel rested, I'll tell you 'bout de chillun. I did n't wan' to write you, fo' both Jim en me know'd 't would mek yu sick. We had to write yu 'bout Jonadab not goin' to school, but Jim en me talked about it, en said we could n't tell yu w'at Jonadab done w'en 'e did n't gone to school.'

Here Chloe stopped as though she had reached a climax, and I was obliged to ask, 'Chloe, what did he do?'

'Miss Pashuns, Jonadab lef' dis ya'd wid 'e book es good en sanctify es any chile kin be, en 'e gone pas' de school een de wood, en 'e stay dere 'till 'bout ten o'clock, den 'e cum home yere wid a gal en a boy en meet Rab, en dem tek de axe en brokee en de house winder, en dey gone through de house, en eat up eberyt'ing dem find, all de can ob tomotus, en de sa-'mon en de sa'dine yu lef' een de closet, dem chillun eat all. Den w'en dey done eat eberyt'ing een de house, dem projek 'round, till dem fin' de store-room key w'ey I had um hide, en dey gone een dey, en tek de meat, en de grits, en de rice, till dem eben carry dem off by de wheel-barrerful down to Elsy en dat 'dulterous man w'at libs wid 'er. I keep a-miss t'ing ebery day, miss t'ing, en miss t'ing, en kyant mek out how de t'ing go so fas', en dem chillun was dat sma't dey hab sense fu' lef' eberyt'ing de look jes' like 'e ain't tech. En de only way I do fu' find out, is w'en yu write de letter fu' tell Jim fu' lick Jonadab, after Jim dun lick um, I 'quisit Dab by himself en I 'quisit Rab by himself, en at last dem confess en tell me de truf.'

I felt perfectly dismayed. I cross-questioned Chloe and felt that there was no doubt of the truth of every word she had uttered; and she looked old and worn, as though by an illness, from the strain.

After giving me time to digest this, and hearing my expressions of disgust and dismay, she went on, 'En den de turkey. When I fus' begin to miss de pee-pee, Miss Vanderbilt had twelve good big one; 'e had had much mo', but dey been a drap off befo' I begin to notice dem dat mo'nin'. I count um keerful, en was jes' a dozen—dat day I lef' Jonadab fu' min' de ya'd till I step down to de plantation en pick de vegetable, en dat night dey was two gone. De nex' day I tek Jonadab wid me en I lef' Rab, en dat time no pee-pee loss, but de nex' day I lef' Dab again en two gone; en ebery time I lef' Dab fu' min' de ya'd I miss two pee-pee, till at las' dere was only seben pee-pee lef', en dat day Rab sick de t'ree dog on Miss Vanderbilt en dem tear she most to pieces en de nex' day him dead, tho' I done all I could fur she.

'Den I say to Jim, "Miss Pashuns mus' see some turkey w'en she come home en I know wha' fu' do."

'Jim say, "Wha' kin yu do?"

'Den I mek answer: "I gwine put de seben pee-pee

een de little coob, en I gwine put de coob een de wheel-barrer en I'll mek Dab roll 'em down to de plantashun."

' "All dat four mile, An' Chloe? Dab kyan't do dat."

'Den I say, "De only way to mek Dab behave 'eself is to keep um stirrin', en I calkilates to stir um dis time."

'So de nex' mo'nin', Miss Pashuns, I put dem seben pee-pee een de coob, en I put de coob een de wheel-barrer, en I mek Jonadab roll dem down to Cherokee, en dat chile was jes' as pleased as if I bin a play wid um. I aimed to lef' de pee-pee down to de plantation dat night een de fowl-house to de ya'd, but w'en I tell Uncl' Bonaparte dat, 'e say, "Yu kyant lef' dem here, fo' I won't tek de 'sponsibility." En I say, "Uncl' Bonaparte I'll lock de fowl-house do' befo' I lef' en yu won't have no 'sponsibility." But Uncl' Bonaparte would n't let me lef' dem, so I had to mek Dab roll dem back, en after dat I jes' kep' it up ebery day I went down to work een de gya'den, en dem seem to prosper.

'But dem chillun keep me drawed out. One day we all sta'ted together en we git 'bout half-way down, en Rab was behind w'en 'e holler to me, "An' Chloe, I have fu' go back, I furgit somethin' "; en befo' I cud say a wud 'e was gone. Dat ebenin' w'en 'e cum, I ax 'im wha' mek 'e stay so long, en 'e tell me say 'e was dat tyad 'e had to lay down ne path to rest. He had a little boy 'e bring wud um, en w'en Rab gone out de chile say, "An' Chloe, Rab neber lay down ne path, Rab gone to Miss Penel'pe sto', en 'e tell Miss Penel'pe say yu sen' um for a box o' red herrin' en say yu say mus' 'scuse yu fu' not come een, but yu'se bery hurry, en yu'se to de gate een de buggy waitin'.' Den Miss Penel'pe wrop up de box quick, en gie um to Rab, en 'e walk out to de road bery fas', en w'en 'e git halfway down 'e brek open de box en 'e eat en 'e gie me some. Den 'e hide de res' in de bush."

'Now yu know, Miss Pashuns, I was shock! W'en Rab come I ax um ef 'e buy herrin' fu' true, en 'e say no, but I ketch 'e han' en smell um en 'e was convict, fu' 'e neber t'ought to wash 'e hand.

'W'en we cum 'long de road dat ebenin' I tell um fu' show me w'ere 'e had de herrin' hide, but 'e wun't. But about a week after dat, one ebenin' 'e say, "An' Chloe, I'll show yu' wey I hide de herrin'," en 'e tek me een de t'icket of bush en sho' me de box, but w'en 'e open um rat or some oder varmint most done eat all. Den 'e offer me one, but I tell um, I neber accept anyt'ing dat is stole.

'Arter dat Rab was bery good fu' a while, but one mo'nin' w'en Dab en me bin a walk purty fas', w'en we git to de gate en I open de gate fu' Dab roll de wheel-barrer trou', 'e look back en 'e say, "An' Chloe, Baby slip us, en gone." I look up de road en I see Rab goin' back as ha'd as 'e kin. Den I walk fas' en mek Dab hurry till we git to de ba'n ya'd en I tu'n de peepee loose, en den we wheel right back en walk fas' fu' ketch Rab, till I begin to blow and Dab say, "An' Chloe, yo'll mek yo'self sick ef yo' walk so fas'; let me run on ahead, en I kin ketch Rab." Den I tell um 'e cud do so, en run on en ketch Rab en fetch um right back to me, en I set down a minit fu' blow, fu' I was plum wore out, but I did n't stop long, en w'en I git to de villige, I fin' my room do' broke open, en my trunk lock broke, en all my t'ing on de flo', en a dollar I had en ten cent, wrop een a piece of silk cloth, was gone, en I could n't fin' neder Rab nor Dab. I put my t'ing 'way as well as I could, en den I wheel right back to de plantation.

'Long 'bout dinner time Jonadab cum bery hurry, en say 'e bin a hunt fu' Rab, but 'e could n't fin' um.

'Miss Pashuns, I was dat discourige 'bout de chillun I was weak, but I hoe out de young tunup, en I try fu' set my min' on scriptur', en I say, "How long, oh Lord, how long!" En arter dat I feel better, but I neber eat a piece o' dinner.

'When sun most down Dab put up de pee-pee, en we gone back to de pineland. W'en Jim cum, en I tell um wha' Rab done, 'e say, I'll gie Rab a lickin' to-night, but w'en sundown cum, we call Rab en we sen' Dab fu' hunt um, but we could n't hear not'ing of um, en I was miserable, en I neber sleep a wink dat night, fu' Rab neber did come till de middle o' the next day, en I was dat glad to see um I would n't let Jim lick um again.

'Two days arter dat, Rab tell me 'e spen' de night right under de big house; say soon as Jim en me gone to bed, 'e mek fire in de chimbley under de house en cook a chicken en a pee-pee en roast two ear o' corn en had a fine supper,—en yo' know, Miss Pashuns, dat was provokin'. When I bin a fret so 'bout de chile, en him bin a eat yo' chicken, en yo' pee-pee, right under yo' own house, en Dab know all de time way him bin, en soon es Jim en me gone to bed, him jump out de winder en jine Rab under de house, en dem cook en eat all night.'

Here Chloe's breath gave out, to my great relief, for this reeling off of the terrible doings of the boys was most distressing. I felt absolutely hopeless. What was the use of struggling with such degenerates? Chloe had been perfectly right, and knew her own race when she warned me of the danger of 'harboring furriners.'

Any one looking at Chloe and then at the boys could

see that they were descendants of different tribes. She was a rich chocolate-brown color, with the regular kinked hair, while the boys were black as ebony, with long straightish hair, and rather aquiline features; they were slender and straight in their build, and the whites of their eyes were very blue. Stanley, in his *Darkest Africa,* describes the great differences in the characteristics of the tribes, some being by nature absolutely honest and others absolutely dishonest. All this I called to mind, and realized that by my own foolhardiness I had taken upon myself two of the worst shoots of one of the very worst African tribes.

During the interval, Chloe had recovered her breath and now began to tell how she had seen Dab deliberately kill with a stick one of the much traveled peepees, so now there were only five.

I interrupted her and said, 'Chloe, I cannot stand another word about the boys. I feel almost distracted already. I have never heard nor dreamed of such creatures! No gratitude, no affection, no fidelity; it is awful, and I do not wonder you look thin and badly. I don't see how you managed to get through at all, and from my heart I thank you for all your efforts. Now I want to beg you not to let the boys know that you have told me all, for I have not the least idea what to do to them as punishment, and yet it is my clear duty to punish them severely; so let them think you have not told me, and to-morrow I will tell them that I cannot give them the suits I brought them from Asheville, as you tell me they have given you a good deal of trouble; but I will give them the mouth organs I brought them.'

I wrung her hand and thanked her again and said, 'Remember, my good Chloe, our Saviour's words, "Inasmuch as ye did it unto the least of these . . . ye did it unto me." '

4

As if to reward me for my leniency, the boys blossomed into wonderful goodness. All their little duties were well and faithfully performed. The turkeys made no more journeys, for I had them rolled down to the plantation the day after my return and put them in the poultry-house, and giving Bonaparte a lock, I told him he must be responsible for them. Every morning Rab donned his clean white apron and churned, one of the regular duties which he had absolutely refused to do during my absence.

In the move from the pineland, Rab and Dab insisted on carrying heavy loads in the wheelbarrow, the only danger being that in their zeal to roll it and their fights over which had had it longest, the freight would suffer. They came and begged me to let them move the 'gereenium' in it, representing that it was much safer for the plant than either the ox-wagon or the horse-cart. I was very much pleased to excite their interest in doing anything well and carefully, so daily I packed as many plants in the little vehicle as it could carry. They took them most successfully. After the move was over, they were very diligent and made the large grounds beautifully clean, one raking up the live-oak leaves, which had fallen during the summer, while the other carted them off to the manure heap in the beloved wheelbarrow.

Jonadab went daily for the mail, proving himself

perfectly reliable in that important function, never stopping to play on the road; so that I had the pleasure of giving them every Saturday evening the nickels which their good conduct brought them, and which they had great joy in spending at Miss Penelope's store for candy, of which they got a surprising amount for the money.

At Christmas I told them to hang up their little socks in the kitchen, but not content with the holding capacity of these they borrowed each a stocking of huge proportions from Chloe, which they hung beside their own. I told Dab to hang up his red socks and Rab his blue pair, so that we should know them apart, for they were very nearly the same size.

By daylight Christmas morning the yard resounded with their shouts of delight and the blasts of their trumpets, horns, and the various instruments of torture to the ear, with which the stockings were filled, besides apples, oranges, peanuts, almonds, raisins, and candy. In the toe of each stocking was a dime. When they came to show me their treasures I gave them the Asheville suits, telling them they had been so good for the past two months that it was a pleasure to give them the new suits and caps.

I was very happy over this beautiful period of calm, and so was Chloe. She said to me one day, 'You see, Miss Pashuns, de Laud sen' yo' dis blessin' to comfort yo', kase yo' loos' all yo' rice crap f'um de freshit, en yo' co'n crap f'um de dry drought, en so 'e won't let Satan worry yo' wid dese chillun, en 'e mek dem good, en dey sure is sarvice to you en to me.'

One day Chloe said to me mysteriously, 'Miss Pashuns, Jonadab tell you anyt'ing?'

'No,' I answered, 'what do you mean?'

Chapter II

Chloe came nearer and said in a low voice, 'Dem see somet'ing.'

'What kind of something, Chloe?'

But Chloe would say nothing more except, 'Ax dem.'

So the first time I had an opportunity of talking to Jonadab alone I said, 'What have you seen strange lately, Jonadab?'

Without the least hesitation he answered, 'A'nt Cinthy.'

'Oh, no, Dab,' I said, 'I know that's not so. When God takes people's souls into the next world they stay there; they do not come back here.'

But Dab was firm, and began to narrate. He had almost lost his stammer now.

'Night befo' las' I bin asleep, en I hear A'nt Cinthy call me, en I open my eye an' dere was A'nt Cinthy fo' true. Him had she head tie wid a w'ite handkerchuff en 'e was all dress in w'ite, wid a bow of black ribbin on she breast, an' she look at me an' Rab very hard, an' I say, "W'at yo' want, A'nt Cinthy?" En him answer, "I wan' me bed, gi' me me bed." En I say, "I ain't got yo' bed." Den she say, "Wey is me bed?" Den I say, "Yo' bed dey een de orcha'd." Den she say, "I wan' me shoe, gi' me me shoe." En I answer, "I ain't got yo' shoe, en I do' kno' wey dem dey." Den she say, "Gi' me me five cent, I wan' me five cent." En I say, "I neber see yo' five cent, go way en le' me 'lone." En den she gone.'

I said, 'Jonadab, you dreamt all this, for Cinthy could not come back if she wanted to, and she would not want to. Where she has gone she has no use for shoes, nor beds, nor five cents, so you may be sure this was a dream.'

I took the earliest opportunity of interviewing Rechab alone, and I asked him a leading question, and he repeated the incident and conversation word for word as Jonadab had done. He told what A'nt Cinthy said and how she looked, laying great stress on the 'bow o' black ribbin on she breast.'

I was quite puzzled over this, but thought it best not to make too much of it, and said nothing more.

At the end of a week Chloe came to me and said, 'Miss Pashuns, we got to do somet'ing. Cinthy do worrit dem po' chillun too much. I know my fault now. I shud 'a bury dat five cent I fin' een a tubacca bag tie tu de head o' de bed, een Cinthy han'. I'll neber ketch een dis trouble agen, I'll know wha' fu' do next time, but de ole lady wha' bin 'e fren', baig fu' de five cent, fu' trow een de chutch, en I gie um to she; en now de po' soul kyant res' un 'e grave, en de my fault. Dab say ebery night, w'en dey de sleep, en de fus' cock crow, she does call um, en some time 'e call Rab. I bin hear people say if you bu'n sulfer een de room dat 'll lay de speret.'

I tried to divert her thoughts from this subject, and began to talk to her about the seasoning of the sausage-meat.

A few days passed and Jim came to me and said, 'Miss Pennington,'—Jim's parents had not belonged to my family, so he does not call me Miss Patience as all the others do,—'I wish you would do something about the boys. Aunt Cinthy has run them clean out o' the house. They don't pertend to sleep there now.'

'Where do they sleep?' I asked.

'In the straw in the loft of the horse stable, ma'am. They bin dere now five nights, en they wun't go back to sleep in their house.'

Chapter II

Chloe came in and added her testimony to Jim's, as to the children's sleeping in the stable; then she added that their poor mother was much to blame in the matter. She said, 'I ax Jonadab, I say, "Yu' ma tell yu' anyt'ing?" 'E say, "No, ma'am, she neber tell me nut-'ing." But Miss Pashuns, dat chile born wid a caul, en ef 'e ma had a mek um swaller de caul, 'e neber 'ood 'a see speret, but long as 'e ma t'row 'way de caul, dat po' chile haf fu' see speret.'

I thought earnestly how I could do anything to reach this situation; then I said, 'I think I know how to quiet the poor spirit; and Jim, I need your help.'

Jim answered with enthusiasm that he was at my command, and I went on, 'Take Jonadab and Rechab and go into the orchard and get Cinthy's bed, and let them each take a corner and help you carry it.'

Jim interrupted, 'It's very light, ma'am; I can carry it myself.'

'I know you can, Jim, but I want you to let each of the boys take a share in carrying it to the burying-ground and placing it over Cinthy's grave, and I am sure the boys will have no more visions of the darkness.'

Jim was very reluctant when he heard this. He said he did n't 'want to meddle in the matter.' But I talked with him about the foolishness of fearing the dead, until he promised to obey my instructions exactly. Whether he did it or not I did not inquire, but I heard no more of Cinthy's nocturnal visits and the children returned to their room quite cheerfully.

CHAPTER III

1

ABOUT the middle of January I was aware that a bad time was coming. Jonadab began to look sulky and stolid, and Jim, when I told him to watch the boys and see what was going wrong, reported that after they had had their supper, said their prayers, and gone to bed, they waited until everything was quiet in the big house, then jumped out of their back window and went out to the 'street,' where they stayed until nearly morning, playing with the other little darkies around big lightwood fires out of doors, or sitting with the grown people around the cabin fires inside.

Plantation Negroes differ from other working people in that they sit up half the night, nodding by the fire, talking, talking, talking, endlessly; they have the 'gift of gab'; but I did not know until now that they let the children sit up just as long as they want to, and just drop asleep anywhere.

I told the boys this must cease; that when they went to bed they must stay there; and I ordered Jim to go to their room the last thing before he went to bed every night. This he did, and as he always found the children fast asleep, I was satisfied.

One day, however, in February, Elihu came and asked to see me privately. I went out and walked into the park some distance from the house, where he could speak without fear of being overheard. He stood hat in hand for some time, and scratched his head before he began.

There are great gradations in the speech of the darkies. Jim speaks quite correctly. Jonadab comes next, and occasionally gets a pronoun right. Chloe's is the rice-field dialect, but somewhat tempered by her association with white people as a house servant. When you hear Elihu you hear the genuine gullah of the rice field, which is harder to understand than the dialect of any other section; and those unaccustomed to it cannot understand a word.

At last he began: 'Miss Pashuns, ma'am, yu'se a lady en I don' like fu' worrit yu', bein' yu'se got no one fu' look out fu' yu'; but, Miss Pashuns, dem chillun yu' got yah is oncommon weekit. Dem is de pu'e Satan, Miss Pashuns. Ebery night de Lawd sen' 'bout twelve o'clock, dem cum to my house en set dere till mawnin', en dem cuss eberybody.'

'Why, Elihu, I can scarcely believe this. I have forbidden them to go out at night, and Jim always goes the last thing at night to see that they are in their beds, and he always finds them asleep.'

'Yes, Miss Pashuns, dem shet dey eye en preten' say dem de sleep, but jes' as soon es Jim shet de do', dem chillun is up en out dat winder. Las' night I say, "Dab," I say, "ent yo' shame, fu' ak so weekit? I gwine tell

Miss Pashuns en 'e'll mek Jim lick yo'." En ma'am, dat boy fu' answer say, "Tell if yu' chuse, en let Jim lick me, en I'll bu'n down de big house, en I'll bu'n down Jim house to-morrer night wen dem de sleep, ef dem lick me." Den Josh bin a set by de fiah, en him jump up, en 'e ketch holt o' Dab en 'e say, "Boy, I'll brek ebery bone in yo' body ef yu' say dat wud agen." En de chillun run out de house en cum home. But I tek it on me, Miss Pashuns, to le' yo' kno' 'bout dey wud, en dey gwinin' on. 'Tain't de fus' time dat I yere dem tretten to stick fiah to dis house en bu'n yu' en An' Chloe up, en dey is dat weekit I 'f'aid sum night dey'll do um.'

'I thank you truly, Elihu. I am glad to know the facts. I have seen that evil thoughts were working in them lately. Poor little creatures, they have to fight a heavier battle with the devil than either you or I, Elihu, and we must try to help them. It was a great thing that Josh spoke so severely to Jonadab for his evil words, and if you will all do that you will help me greatly; but I hear some of the people only laugh at what they say, and encourage them to say worse. I really do not know what to do as long as you receive them into your houses at night and let them stay there and talk and laugh, when you know that it is against my express orders and that they ought to be in their beds. Now, if you will tell all the people in the street that I beg them not to allow the boys to enter their houses after ten o'clock, you will be doing me a favor, and perhaps I shall be able to keep them in their beds. Go round as soon as you get home and tell the head of each house in the street that I require this of them.'

I consulted both Chloe and Jim as to what could be

done, but no plan could be devised, except that which I had proposed—of getting the help of the hands on the place; and for a time it seemed to succeed.

One Sunday morning after breakfast, Chloe called me out to the yard, where, under a large oak, on the top-most limb of which he always roosted, lay the peacock, dead, a tumbled mass of gorgeous colors. I was very much distressed, and still more so when I had heard Chloe's account. The boys had 'chunked' it to death.

She said that when she first got up that morning she heard them laughing very loud and 'chunking' with brickbats. She went out to see what they were doing, and found that they were throwing things at the peacock, which was on a very high limb. She scolded them and made them stop, and then went into the house to carry fresh water; and when she came down, they had gone to the barnyard. She looked up into the tree and saw the peacock still sitting high up on a limb, and she knew he was afraid to come down. She went on with her duties, and thought no more of it until a few moments ago, when she heard the loud laughing again, and ran out just in time to see the beautiful bird fall to the ground dead; a brick had struck him on the head.

I questioned Jonadab, who was standing by. He said that he never 'chunked' the peacock, that it had eaten too much and dropped dead in the night; and so on and on, telling one lie after another with extraordinary glibness and ingenuity. I turned to Rechab with the same result. I was very angry. I sent for Jim and told him to give them both a good whipping.

Jonadab fought Jim desperately, so that his hands had to be tied, to prevent his scratching Jim's face and

Chapter III 53

tearing his clothes. While Jonadab was receiving his punishment at the old school-house some distance from the house, I talked to Rechab with all the eloquence that I could command, shaming him for his wickedness and telling him what the end of it all must be, and urging him to tell the truth, which at last he did, and confessed the whole thing.

When Jim brought Jonadab back and took Rechab, I told him to make his punishment lighter as he had made confession. Fortunately, Jonadab's hands were still tied, for as soon as Jim had gone off with Rab he broke out into the most fearful oaths and threats of killing and burning and then running off into the swamp.

I was sorely puzzled to know what to do with him. It was time to start for church, a long drive, and as I could not leave him in this frame of mind, I told Chloe to bring the key to the basement, which used to be the pastry kitchen in former years; it was all of brick, with an immense brick oven and fireplace, and the windows had thick bars instead of shutters; so I had Jonadab put in there until I returned from church.

There was nothing in the basement but some old pieces of furniture and the barrel of kerosene oil, which was always kept there with a locked spigot; so there was nothing for him to destroy. As he continued to threaten to burn and kill, I left his hands bound, examining carefully to see that there was nothing to hurt him.

I found it very difficult to fix my mind on holy things when I got to church, and I did not benefit from the blessed services as much as usual, for the events of the morning had agitated and shaken me, and I felt that I must decide upon some steps at once, to secure better management for Jonadab. I had done my very best for the boys, giving them of my time and thought, but they had come to a point where they did not improve and I must make some change. They were growing in health and strength and capacity, but morally not at all. For two years we had suffered from disastrous freshets which had destroyed my rice crop, and I had not had a dollar to spend and had bought not a single thing of any kind for myself, but I must manage to do something for Jonadab.

I hurried home as soon as the service was over, without the usual little chat with my kindly friends and neighbors, who live so far apart and lead such busy lives that we rarely meet elsewhere. I told Jim to drive rapidly home, and I hurried to the basement to release Jonadab. I spoke to him most earnestly and solemnly, and making him kneel down, I knelt beside him and made him repeat after me a fervent prayer that God would deliver him from the evil spirit which tempted him, and help him to be a good boy. At last Jonadab seemed to be softened, and to feel some regret for his conduct, and promised to do better; and I went into the house exhausted, but much more cheerful than I had been.

2

That night I wrote three letters; one to Booker Washington, as the wisest of his race, asking him if he could tell me of a place where I could send these orphans, where they would be kindly cared for, and at the same time have the regular, disciplined life which alone could save them from their inherited evil proclivities. Then I wrote to the reverend archdeacon for

Chapter III

colored work in our diocese, asking him the same question. Then to the rector of my parish, a man who had devoted himself a great deal to work among the Negroes in former years. I wrote very freely to him, stating the circumstances and asking if he knew of any institution or any individual to whom I could intrust these children. I told each one that I was prepared to bear their expenses entirely myself, but I hoped they would be moderate, as my means were small.

The next day Chloe came to me in dismay. 'Miss Pashuns, yu' know dis karisene only cum last week, en I git out two gallon, en now de barrel is empty!'

'That is impossible, Chloe; the barrel holds over fifty gallons.'

'I know dat, Miss Pashuns, but I'm tellin' yu' now, de barrel is empty, en de flo' is deep in karisene; look a' my shoe.'

I looked and truly Chloe's shoes were wet with kerosene. I went at once to the basement to examine, and found it was all true: Jonadab had broken the locked spigot with a piece of old iron he found, and when I was talking to him so earnestly the day before, the oil was quietly flowing out of the barrel. The room was dark and I had stood near the door; and I was so engrossed with the effort to impress the child that, though I had been aware of the strong smell of kerosene, I made no investigation, having no suspicion. I had noticed that his hands were free, and when I asked him how he loosed them, he said he went close to the window and Rab had loosed them by putting his hands through the bars. I was pleased that he told me the truth, and did not think it remarkable. I never had been forced to have such a thing done to any child before, and the thought of it had worried me all during service, and when I found that Rab had loosed him I was rather glad than otherwise.

The basement floor being tiled, the oil was still there, and I told Chloe to try to dip some up; but of course it did not amount to anything, and I had to sit down at once and write to C. for another barrel of vestal oil. It would cost $9.80 by the time freight was paid, and I should have to wait a week to get it by the next steamer.

I never mentioned the subject to Jonadab, feeling it would do no good, unless I had him punished again, which I was not willing to do. I had done all I could, and I simply ignored this new wickedness.

Meanwhile I watched the mail eagerly for answers to my letters. In due time they came. Booker Washington 'was sorry he knew of no institution where boys so young could be placed. His own were all for larger boys.' The reverend archdeacon answered that he regretted beyond measure the fact that there was no place for just such cases; it was a great need all over the country. My rector gave the same answer, while expressing great interest and sympathy.

Every day some fresh ingenuity of naughtiness on the part of the boys came to light, and I tried to meet it with some fresh idea to divert them from evil.

Their parents had both been Baptists, and as I had a feeling that their poor mother would prefer their being brought up in her own faith, I had never had them baptized into the church; but now I felt that I had been wrong, and I had them both christened in our little chapel for colored people, the bishop, the archdeacon, and the rector all being present. It was a very solemn service and I felt very hopeful of the result, having a blessed faith in the power of the Holy Spirit.

Chapter III

I had often read in the *News and Courier* of the work of a Negro man named Jenkins in the town of Charleston, who had begun by picking up little waifs of his race on the streets, taking them to his own home, and caring for them as if they were his own children, making them respectable and law-abiding by his excellent management and discipline, so that all the citizens of Charleston had become interested in his work and had given him their help and encouragement; until at last the city had given him the use of a big building, where he now had a large number of children under his training and care.

I wrote to my sister, whose home is in that town, and begged her to visit the Jenkins establishment, and let me know what she thought of it.

While I was waiting for her report, Jim came to me one day with a very serious face, and said, 'Miss Pennington, Jonadab bin in my room, in my top drawer, an' took out all my cartridge, about twenty I had, an' done shot um off in the fire at night to their house! Now w'en he bin into the sto'room an' took pervision, an' into An' Chloe's trunk an' broke it open an' took her money, I never t'ought nothin' of that, fo' all chillun will do such t'ings, but w'en it come to that, that Jonadab got sense to go into my drawer an' take cartridge an' shoot dem off in the fire, I t'ink it's time fo' somet'ing to be done.'

I could not help smiling at the fact that in Jim's opinion his own loss was the only serious one, but I said, 'I heartily agree with you, Jim. It is quite time for something to be done, and I am trying my best to find out what it must be. In the meantime keep your eye on Jonadab all the time, for there is no telling what he may do.'

My sister's report of the Jenkins institution was most satisfactory. She had been all through it, had seen the children at work and at play, and Jenkins himself impressed her with confidence.

I wrote at once to him, asking if he would take Jonadab. Very soon came his reply,—that he did not ordinarily take children outside of the city, as he found so many in it that needed his care; but that I had interested him in the boy, and he would receive him and do the best he could for him.

I had been busy all along making up new clothes for Jonadab, and got a best suit for his Sunday wear from Gregory, so that there was no cause for delay.

I called Jonadab the next morning and told him I was going to take him to school. He was delighted, and when his little valise was packed and he got into the wagon with it, he was bursting with importance and pride. He seemed to feel no shadow of regret in leaving Rechab, but called out in a joyful tone as the wagon drove off, 'Goodbye, Baby.' But poor Rab looked very sad.

I felt considerable anxiety as to how Jonadab would behave on the journey: he had so often threatened to 'run away' that I half feared he might try something of the sort; but I soon saw he was in one of his very best moods. During the fourteen-mile drive to the station, he looked at everything with intense pleasure and asked Jim, by whose side he sat, endless questions.

When we reached the station I got at once into the train and placed Jonadab on the little side seat near the door, with his own little valise and my suitcase by him, and told him to take care of them and not to move till I came for him; and I took my seat at a little distance.

Chapter III

There he sat like an ebony statue, not moving a muscle; but his eyes rolled around in the most wonderful way, and saw everything. He had never seen a town, or a car, or a locomotive; he had never seen anything in his life but the sights of the country, the little pineland settlement called a village, with one store, a post-office, and a church, set down irregularly among the tall pines; yet there was no expression of surprise or wonder,—just an all-devouring interest.

A stranger who sat behind me leaned over and said, 'Pardon me, but I saw you speak to that little boy; do you know him?'

Of course I answered in the affirmative, and the stranger went on: 'He is a very extraordinary-looking child. He would make his fortune as a minstrel; he is a typical minstrel darkie.'

We did not reach the city until ten o'clock, and I had to take a carriage in order to reach the Jenkins Industrial Institution, for I had no idea how to get there on the trolley. The nephew who met me at the train urged me to take Jonadab to his mother's for the night, saying that in the morning I could take him to the worthy Jenkins without the expense of a carriage; but I was not to be dissuaded from carrying out my original intention of placing Jonadab in Jenkins's care that night; so, giving the hackman the address, we drove off.

A fair for the benefit of the orphans was in full blast when we arrived and the place looked very gay. There was some delay in finding the principal, but finally he came to the carriage and I had the satisfaction of placing my charge in safe hands. I was pleased, too, with Jenkins's appearance and his manner toward his new responsibility. Knowing that Jonadab had never seen anything like the gorgeousness of the flag-trimmed fair room, I was glad that he should have such a gay impression of his new home, and gave him three nickels to spend as he pleased. I arranged with the principal to go the next day and make the necessary business arrangements, and then I was free to enjoy the meeting with my loved ones.

The next day Jenkins told me that if I gave up all hold on Jonadab, that is, all control for the future, I need pay nothing, but if I desired still to be responsible for him I must pay a small sum twice a year for his board and clothing, which sum I paid down at once. Then I was taken all over the large establishment, which seemed wonderfully well organized and managed, the children well fed and clothed and happy, and yet all busy.

I felt it necessary to tell Jenkins of Jonadab's propensities, at the same time asking him to appear not to know them, so as to give the child a chance to forget them and make a fresh start, and above all not to let any of his companions know them. The old adage, 'Give a dog a bad name and hang him,' is founded on a knowledge of human nature.

On the train, once, I had asked Dab if he had ever thought what he would like to be when he grew up,—what work he would like to do. He had answered without hesitation, 'Engineer on a steamboat,' and I told Jenkins that.

I was much impressed by the quiet common sense of Jenkins, and by his ability. I asked to see Dab before I left and found him radiantly happy, and I returned home with a quiet mind, feeling that I had found the place where the best part of Jonadab would be developed.

3

When I got back to Cherokee, a very clean, very good little Rechab met me. Chloe had taken him into her hands more than when Jonadab had been at home, and Jim had had him to sleep in his room. Jim, however, was often away, and so I told Chloe I wanted Rab to sleep in one of the small rooms off her room, as I wanted him looked after especially at night, so that there should be no chance of his relapsing into the habit of nocturnal wandering. To my great surprise Chloe did not seem willing, and at last she said, 'Miss Pashuns, Rab is a bery peepin' chile, en I kyant hab him een dat closet wid de curtin, rite next to me.'

So I sent for Bonaparte and told him to make a door at once and put it up between Chloe's room and the little room, and to put a bolt on the outside so that Chloe could control and defeat Rab's peeping proclivities. Without Jonadab's leading spirit, Rab seemed likely to become a model boy. I took him with me, whenever it was possible, behind the buckboard to open gates and hold the horse when I made visits. I questioned him about things and encouraged him to talk, hoping thus to aid his unconscious development. As a great treat Saturday evening, I let him go to the 'street' to play with the children, but required him to be back at ten o'clock. One day when I was driving I asked him what they talked about in the street the night before, when he went there. He answered promptly,—

'Dem tell me how fu' get money out a bank.'

'What kind of bank, Rab?'

'I don' mean no rice-field bank, Miss Pashuns, I mean a bank w'ere dem keep money.'

'But how is it possible to get money out of that kind of bank, Rab?'

'Fust t'ing, Miss Pashuns, yu' must kill a eagle, en de eagle got a little stone in 'e hed, en yu' mus' tek out dat stone, en yu' mus' carry um to de bank winder wey de glass dey, en yu' mus' hold um up to de winder, en 'e'll draw de money right out o' dat bank, into yo' pocket.'

I feared that poor little Rab's character was not likely to be elevated by his Saturday evening outings.

After six months I heard that Jonadab was a member of the 'Celebrated Jenkins Band,' which had played before the crowned heads of Europe,—before Dab entered it, be it added,—and Jim and Chloe were filled with pride at the news, and Rab devoted more time than ever to practice on the mouth-organ.

At the end of the year, when I sent the second payment to Jenkins, asking to know particularly how Jonadab was getting on, I received a most cheering answer. Dab was well and happy, and perfectly satisfactory in every way to the principal. Rechab seemed also to have entered the straight and narrow way, and I felt that my decision to separate the boys had been a wise one, and, I trusted, had come in time to save them both.

I found, however, that Rab had not half the character that Jonadab had evinced in certain things. He was now as old as Jonadab had been when he began to carry the mail, but it was impossible to trust the mail to Rab; he would meet children on the road, and throw the mail-bag down and enter into either a fight or a game, more often the first.

I sent him to school and he fought each child in the school in turn; sometimes he got badly beaten, but he easily forgot that in the many more victories he had.

Chapter III

At last Miss Somerville told me that she could do nothing with him; that he kept the schoolroom in such turmoil that order was impossible; that when the children were marching round in their little drill, Rab would skillfully extend one foot and trip up one after another, and a lively fight would ensue.

After listening to this report, I said, 'Then perhaps I had better take Rab away from school'; and Miss Somerville answered, 'I will be very much obliged if you will.'

Then I told Rab that he must bring his books to me every day and I would teach him; but he has so many ways of skillfully evading, that it is hopeless in the busy life I lead to keep him to it. The worst feature is his insolence to Chloe and Gerty, my housemaid. In speaking to people outside he says, 'I got cook en I got washer. Chloe 'blige to cook fu' me and Gerty 'blige to wash for me.' This he says when I am away. It rouses all the powers of evil in my excellent Chloe, and I see hanging over me the moment when she will say that she 'can't hold out no longer,' and I shall be left alone with Rab. So now I am diligently seeking a place to put him where he will have the proper discipline from one of his own race.

This winter he behaved so outrageously that punishment was necessary. I told Chloe the thing had to be done, even if she had to get help, for alas Jim is no longer with me. So Chloe and Gerty, with the assistance of another 'free male,' as Chloe pronounces it, succeeded in holding down Rab and giving him a whipping. It did him a great deal of good for about ten days, but after that he narrated for the benefit of the street how it took 't'ree woman' to lick him, and then he gave a careful and detailed account of the whole thing, to the hilarious amusement of his audience.

Of course when Chloe heard this, she was most indignant, and vowed that she had done with Rechab and would never speak to him again,—which made things very uncomfortable for a time. But fortunately that phase passed after a while.

This summer after we moved to the pineland, Rab took to sleeping out, just dropping in for his meals whenever it suited him, in a casual way, with all the airs of a dissipated young man. I tried everything possible to bring him to order, for I found he spent the nights with a man who is a regular thief, and always on the ragged edge of conviction,—a punishment which he escapes because his wife works and pays off for him; that is, offers the people whose fields have been robbed so much to drop the case. I knew what a valuable tool to such a person Rab would be.

At one time he was gone three days, and I heard he spent all the time with these people. So I drove to the woman's house, and leaving Gerty to hold my buggy in the road, went to the house and knocked. When the woman opened the door, I went in a little way and told her I had come to beg her not to let Rab stay in her house all the time, but always to send him home after he had made her a short visit.

She was very polite and humble in her manner, and assured me that Rab had not been near her; that she had no idea where he stayed, for it was not with her.

I was quite disarmed and went back to the buggy, feeling that I had been misinformed. But as I took my seat I said, 'Gerty, have you been looking around to see if you can see anything of Rab?'

She answered, 'I never haf' to look, ma'am; just as you gone in de do' Rab jump out de winder and run into de woods.'

Chapter III

That afternoon, just as the dark was falling, the dogs began to make a great noise, and I looked up from my book to see a strange man, with about thirty feet of rope wound around his body and arm, walking into the yard holding a small black figure by the shoulder. The scene was most dramatically arranged. It was Rab being led back by the hardened sinner, Bob, whose guest he had been during his three days' absence.

I continued to read until they reached the step; then I looked up and said, 'What is this?'

'De me, Bob, ma'am, I fetch Rab back to you, en I got rope tu tie um.'

'I don't want Rab,' I said; 'I certainly won't keep any one with me that has to be tied. Take him back with you. I don't want him.'

There was a profound silence, during which I read on; then I looked up again and said, 'Take him back with you,' once more.

Then I heard a subdued sniffle from Rab and a mumbled, 'I won't do so no more, Miss Pashuns.'

'I have heard that too often, Rab. I have struggled with you a long time, and put up with a great deal because I promised your poor mother to take care of you; but when it comes to your running away and having to be brought back by a man with yards of rope wrapped round him, I can't stand it. You must go and find your home elsewhere.'

By this time Rab was weeping openly and said, 'Please, Miss Pashuns, don' sen' me 'way; I wan' fu' stay wid you! I don' want to lib no way else; please, ma'am, le' me stay. I wunt run 'way no more.'

So finally I consented to try him a little longer, and dismissed Bob and his dramatic coil of rope.

This was all a great big bluff on my part, and I kept

wondering all the time what I should do if Rab cheerfully turned and walked away with Bob, for I could not free myself from the feeling of responsibility for him.

Being almost in despair, I am writing in every direction to find a safe place for Rab. When I took him he was four. He is now eleven. My only consolation is that faith of which I have spoken before, that good must in the end triumph.

That faith seems to have been justified in Jonadab's case, for when I went to the Institute this spring, to see him and inquire as to his conduct, Jenkins was not at home, but the next in control saw me and said,—

'Jonadab is our very best boy. When we have anything hard that we want done, we call on him and he never disappoints us.'

So I struggle on with poor little Rab, hoping that the terrible battle within him will end in victory to the good spirit.

EPILOGUE

Rab and Dab Up-to-Date

THERE have been so many requests to know what has become of Rab and Dab that I am giving a short account of what happened next.

As the time came near for Dab's four years with the worthy Jenkins to be out, I began to plan eagerly for Rab's entrance to the Institute. I felt it was most important that the brothers should not meet, for the motto 'united we stand, divided we fall' could certainly be reversed in their case; they could not be together without falling, and Dab having won so high a character, I was reluctant to subject it to so great a strain. While I was debating in my own mind how I could dispose of Dab while I introduced Rab to the Jenkins Orphan Institute, for they were naturally eager to meet (and poor little Rab talked constantly of the great things they would do 'w'en my bubber Jesse come home'), I received a letter from my sister in the mountains asking if I would let her have Jonadab for the summer as she needed a boy. It seemed really almost an answer to prayer. I wrote her I would send him with delight, and the simple preparations began.

I was overjoyed at this solution of my problem; if I had hunted the world over, I could not have found one with a greater gift for training animals and children than my sister. Her dogs and horses have always been models, and whenever a child has been spending a few months with her, it has always been a good child, regardless of its former history. To have my poor little stuttering, pock-marked Dab committed to her care and training was a real blessing. Besides, she had in her employ as general major domo Roger, a thoroughly trained house servant and a good man, and I knew that being of the same race, he could influence Dab as no one of another race could. So Dab bid farewell to the Institute and, with his little belongings packed in a small trunk given him by my dear D., made the journey to the mountains.

I looked anxiously for the first letter for I knew that the Master of the household at the Lodge, being an Englishman and partial to a quiet well-ordered establishment, had been rather dismayed when he heard of the proposed addition to the ménage, having perhaps heard too many anecdotes from Dab's former career. I was, however, fully occupied getting Rab established at the Jenkins Orphan Institute. As soon as Dab got off, I took Rab down to Charleston and placed him with the worthy Jenkins. The journey was bliss to Rab—he was indeed a whole minstrel show in himself. When he reached the great big brick house and found it was full of boys, and that he could fight to his heart's content if he only did not break the rules, he asked no more of Life as the food was abundant. The big gates were always open but he was told if he went out he would find himself in the hands of the police. That was

Epilogue

the greatest terror that the world held for him, because it was something unknown, and I felt sure Rab would not take French leave, at least not for a long time. I left him feeling that the best would be done for him.

The first letter I got from the Lodge told that the morning after Dab's arrival, as the Master strolled around the garden after breakfast, he saw on the porch a fine large rat-trap of the newest pattern. It happened that they had had great trouble with rats in the stable and had not been able to get an efficient trap, so the Master was delighted at the sight of this up-to-date and competent looking article. He called the Mistress and congratulating her upon it, asked where she got it. She looked at it in great surprise, and said she knew nothing about it. At this moment Dab appeared with beaming face and with his best and most prolonged stutter said to the Master, ' 'Tis me pres—ent um to yu sah! I bring um frum Chastun fur yu sah.' It was so entirely unexpected, and at the same time so very apropos, that Dab was established on a new footing at once, and showed himself very useful as well as docile. Roger was very good to him and taught him all that he could, and it was a blissful summer to him. L. had some of the children of the family staying with her and one day she heard from the sitting-room window this dialogue: 'Dab, how much wages does Aunt L. give you?'

'I don' kno', I don' keer ef she don' gie me notting; I'se *too* happy!'

Dab's resourceful mind became a great joke; no one could stump him—for every problem he found a ready solution, and it became the Master's unvarying answer, when asked what to do under trying and unexpected circumstances, 'Ask Dab,' and sure enough

Dab stuttered out some ingenious way out of the difficulty.

From the time his regular duties were shown and explained to him, he was as regular as the sun in their performance at the proper time, never having to be reminded to do them.

So I also had a quiet happy summer. . . .

A NOTE ON THE TEXT

Though Elizabeth Allston Pringle worked on various versions of the story of Rab and Dab for more than a decade, only one complete version appears to have survived: the *Atlantic Monthly* serial text. There is an incomplete manuscript, entitled "Rab and Dab the Orphans," in her papers at the South Carolina Historical Society in Charleston. (See illustration.) It differs sufficiently from the *Atlantic* text to make clear that at least one later version must have been written.

On January 28, 1908, in a letter to the historian Frederic Bancroft, Mrs. Pringle thanks him for his "kind offer to take the m.s. of the orphans and introduce it to the notice of Mr. McClure" (Bancroft Collection, Columbia University Library). If Bancroft submitted it to the editor of *McClure's Magazine* it was rejected. That version may have been called "The Deuce"—an apt title, since we can assume she knew both its contemporary secondary meaning of a mild oath, and the older one: bad luck. In a letter to Bancroft of September 4, 1908, she thanks him for "taking so much trouble for me . . . to make 'The Deuce' available."

The change in title indicates that it was a later version, then, which went to the *Atlantic,* though there is no way of telling how much she may have revised it. In a letter to Bancroft dated August 27, 1914, she asks him to send her "the ms of 'Rab & Dab' which you have been so kind in having typed for me and then keeping all this time—I had almost forgotten about it, but now a part is to come out in the Atlantic Monthly of November and I want to make a few alterations, and instead of type writing it myself I remembered that you had told me you had a copy put away—"

Presumably this typescript became setting copy for the *Atlantic* text but no trace of it, or of the manuscript from which it was made, survives among Mrs. Pringle's papers. Nor are there in her surviving correspondence any letters to or from the *Atlantic*—which might have revealed whether or not she was able to see proofs of the work.

The text of *Rab and Dab* published here, then, with the exception of the epilogue, is taken from the three-part serial version published in the *Atlantic Monthly:* vol. 114, no. 5 (November 1914), pp. 577–589; vol. 114, no. 6 (December 1914), pp. 799–808; vol. 115, no. 1 (January 1915), pp. 90–98. Only one editorial emendation has been made: the choice of consistently spelling her pen name as it is pronounced by the blacks, in the Gullah fashion, "Miss Pashuns" rather than "Miss Patience." Though in the original text this usage varies from one serial installment to another, bringing the work out in book form called for a greater degree of consistency, and the Gullah version appears more frequently and best fits the linguistic form of the dialogue. In addition a few obvious misprints, and several errors and irregularities in punctuation were corrected. However, no attempt was made to impose a

Note on Text

greater degree of uniformity upon the spelling or punctuation of the dialect passages. Her manuscripts reveal that Mrs. Pringle was concerned to indicate a great deal of variety in the speech of her black characters—variety in pronunciation, rhythm, tone, and emphasis, and she attempted to give some idea of this by variations in spelling, contraction, and punctuation.

The epilogue—though she did not call it this—was found among her papers at the South Carolina Historical Society. It exists in three separate typescript drafts in various stages of completion. The text published here combines the most finished and developed parts of all three versions, under the title "Rab and Dab up to Date," which she gave to what is apparently the last version. (An earlier version is entitled "The Regeneration of Rab and Dab.") Obvious typing errors have been corrected, and spelling and punctuation have occasionally been modified to conform with the *Atlantic* text.

A.B.